**"Hey!" she protested. "I thought this was supposed to be *touch* football?"**

"Exactly," he whispered against her neck. His hold tightened, his strong hands spanning her waist, his fingers inches from her breasts. Before she could utter a protest, Cedric's lips connected with the one spot on her neck that drove her mindless.

Payton gasped with need, covering the arms that latched around her and throwing her head back to give him better access. Still locked together, Cedric shuffled their bodies over to the wall. He turned her around and pinned her against it, then zeroed in on her neck again, kissing and licking and nipping his way up and down.

He found her breast. Despite the layers of clothing separating his hand and her skin, her body's reaction couldn't have been stronger if they were both naked. Her nipple puckered, instantly drawing tight. Her skin burned from the inside out.

Cedric released her neck from his erotic assault. His hand continued to caress her breast as he stared into her eyes, seeking permission. With a slight nod, Payton put an end to both their miseries.

Permission granted.

**Books by Farrah Rochon**

Kimani Romance

*Huddle with Me Tonight*
*I'll Catch You*

---

## FARRAH ROCHON

had dreams of becoming a fashion designer as a teenager, until she discovered she would be expected to wear something other than jeans to work every day. Thankfully, the coffee shop where she writes does not have a dress code.

When Farrah is not penning stories, the avid sports fan feeds her addiction to football by attending New Orleans Saints games.

# I'LL
# *Catch You*

## FARRAH ROCHON

KIMANI™
ROMANCE

For my Dreadnaughts,
I cannot imagine my life without all of you.

"A friend loves at all times…" —*Proverbs* 17:17

KIMANI PRESS™

ISBN-13: 978-0-373-86203-0

I'LL CATCH YOU

Recycling programs
for this product may
not exist in your area.

Dear Reader,

Do you remember those days when there was a clear line between a man's and a woman's work? As we forge ahead into the twenty-first century, that line has become blurred, but there are still a few careers that lean heavily toward male dominance. The sports agent profession is one of them. Being the type of person who loves to push the envelope, I just knew I *had* to have a female sports agent.

When creating the heroine in *I'll Catch You,* Payton Mosely, I wanted to devise a character who was smart and strong enough to thrive in this male-dominated profession, yet also feminine enough to knock the hero, Cedric Reeves, off his feet. I think I accomplished both. I think you'll agree that the chemistry between these two really sizzles.

I hope you enjoy this second glimpse into the world of the New York Sabers football team. Get ready for teammates Jared Dawson and Theo Stokes, whose stories are coming soon, and be sure to check out Torrian's story, the first in the Sabers series, in *Huddle With Me Tonight.*

Don't be a stranger! Visit me at www.farrahrochon.com or seek me out on Facebook and Twitter. I love hearing from readers!

All the best,

Farrah Rochon

## Acknowledgments

Special thanks to Susan Renee Sutphen for contributing to Brenda Novak's Diabetes Auction.

Thanks to my uncle, Terry Roybiskie, for his insights into the game of football.

To my aunt, Dr. Madeline Borne. Belated thanks for your help in coming up with the perfect eye ailment for Torrian.

# Chapter 1

The aroma of sweat and dirt blended with a myriad of expensive colognes, creating a nauseating odor that suffused the locker room and clung to Payton Mosely's nostrils.

Payton tamped down the urge to pull her shirt over her nose. None of the other reporters seemed affected by the overpowering smells attacking her olfactory system with the force of the entire New York Sabers defensive line. They were used to this, and if she wanted to maintain her facade long enough to accomplish her goal, she had to suck it up and deal.

She ducked and weaved her way through the crowd of reporters wearing press passes identical to the one that hung around her neck. The names printed on theirs probably matched the names on their driver's licenses, something Payton could not claim. Today she was Susan Renee Sutphen, sports writer for the *Buffalo Daily*.

Nothing short of a full day of pampering at a day spa would be suitable to thank Sue for allowing Payton to use her press pass. If she was caught, Sue's paper would likely be banned from the Sabers locker room. And that was the best scenario. Her friend could lose her job over this.

The crush of reporters surrounding the Sabers's punt-return specialist, Jared Dawson, whose ninety-eight-yard kick return for a touchdown set a Sabers record and sealed today's victory against the Philadelphia Eagles, slowed her forward momentum, but Payton would not be deterred. She wasn't here to get a quote from the game winner. She would never put up with this stink for something as simple as a recap of today's football game. Payton had her sights set on a much bigger prize, and she was going to be waiting at his locker for him.

He emerged from the shower room, bare-chested, with sweatpants that hung low on his waist.

Cedric Reeves.

Payton's steps halted. That confidence she'd been building over the course of the game needed a pep talk before approaching the man who would make or break her career, especially if she had to go near him in his current state of undress. He had a running back's body, solid and strong, without an ounce of visible fat lurking, only muscle and a whole lotta attitude.

Dark brown skin glistened over the rippling muscles of his supremely defined abs. The six-pack looked as if it had been created by a master sculptor with the sole purpose of driving the female population crazy.

Payton's palms itched with the urge to glide across all that glorious skin but she reined in the impulse. She wasn't here to admire his physique; she was here to convince Cedric Reeves to become the first client of Mosely Sports Management. Despite the stomach-turning affects of the pungent locker-room air, she sucked in a deep breath and used one of the pranayama breathing techniques she'd learned in yoga class to calm her rapid heartbeat.

This was it: make or break time. Two possible outcomes: either she convinced the Sabers running back to take her on as his new agent, or she threw her dream in the gutter and headed back to West Texas.

Payton tossed away that idea before the image of tumbleweed could roll through her psyche. The only thing that would take her back to her small hometown was a visit with her mother. Her life was here, in New York. And her profession was sports agenting.

All she needed was a client.

"All or nothing, Mosely," she whispered under her breath.

Payton's eyes zeroed in on Cedric. He stood before a wooden alcove that sported his name engraved on a teal nameplate above it. The locker room contained about eighty identical cubbyholes made of a beautiful solid oak, gleaming, as if the wood had been polished by hand. They made a semicircle around the room, each with a cushioned folding chair in that same Sabers teal that was the color of choice for just about everything at Sabers Stadium.

A couple of reporters surrounded Cedric with their various recording devices shoved in his face. There was too much noise for Payton to hear what he was saying, but he either made quick work of answering their questions or blew them off, because within a few minutes they were gone.

Payton took another deep breath, straightened her shoulders and walked with a confidence born of countless mini-pep talks like the one she'd just given herself. Just as she approached Cedric, another reporter stepped in front of her and stuck a voice recorder in the running back's face.

"Any truth to the rumored meeting you had with the Sabers general manager, Cedric?"

Cedric tossed the towel he'd had around his shoulders onto the floor and pulled a platinum herringbone chain over his head. A diamond-studded cross lay in the center of his chest, gleaming from the florescent lights that tracked along the locker room's ceiling.

"The key word there is rumored," was Cedric's answer as he pulled on a long-sleeved T-shirt and covered up that beautiful chest. The shirt couldn't hide the well-defined muscles of his arms and shoulders, though.

Salivating over his body was *so* not the right thing to do at the moment. She had to be professional.

"Come on, Reeves," the reporter continued. "It's common knowledge that your agent dropped you after that incident with the fan in Baltimore. Word is the Sabers are looking to do the same."

"As much as I would love to spend the next three hours talking about this, I'm due for a massage with one of the trainers. I'm sure you saw the nasty hit I took at the end of the third quarter." He retrieved an alligator-skin duffel bag from the base of the locker, then turned in the direction of the shower and training rooms where the press was not allowed.

Payton intercepted him before he could take another step. "Mr. Reeves, can I have a word with you?"

His shoulders stiffened as he turned. "I just said 'no more'—" he raised his head and after a pause finished "—questions." His eyes widened with interest as they traveled from her head to her feet. Despite being fully clothed, Payton felt as naked as a stripper at the end of her pole-dance routine.

Cedric ended his perusal at her face, then he squinted. His forehead creased in a deep vee and he pointed at her. "Don't I know you?"

"Not really," Payton answered, her shored-up confidence washing out to sea with that one accusing question.

"Yes, I do. You're that agent chick who's been stalking me."

Payton's eyebrows shot up in indignant surprise. "I have *not* been stalking you."

"No? What would you call it?" He ticked a list off on his fingers. "You've emailed me about a dozen times, called the Sabers front offices and tried to trick the receptionist into giving you my cell number and friended me on Facebook. Nice profile picture, by the way. Although it doesn't do you justice."

Payton felt her face heating. Listening to a detailing of her activities over the past few weeks, she thought she did sound a little stalkerish.

He leaned in closer and read her press pass. "And now you're pretending to be a reporter. Where's Susan Renee Sutphen? Locked up in the trunk of your car?"

Payton had known her ruse would be discovered as soon as he spotted her, but it had gotten her what she wanted, face time with Cedric Reeves. She figured she had about a minute to make her pitch, and she wasn't going to waste another second of it.

"The only reason I resorted to this is because you've ignored all of my other attempts to contact you," she said.

"Most people would take the hint," he replied.

"Is there a reason you refuse to talk to me? I may be just the agent you've been looking for."

"What makes you think I'm looking for an agent?"

Payton quelled the impulse to roll her eyes, frustrated but not surprised by his reluctance to even admit he needed her.

"It's common knowledge that you and Gus Houseman have parted ways, and that you haven't been able to find another agent willing to take you on."

He folded his arms across his broad chest and leveled her with a stare that said loud and clear he wasn't happy with her assessment of his situation, but Payton surged forward.

"It's also common knowledge that you become a free agent at the end of the season, but other teams haven't been biting."

"Wow, sounds like I'm the talk around the watercooler. Tell me, what else have the Common Knowledge Guys said about me?"

"I'm being dead serious, Mr. Reeves. If you go into negotiations with the Sabers unagented, you're going to get screwed. That is, if they negotiate with you at all." Payton stepped up to him and got right in his face. "You need me."

Several moments passed before he barked out a laugh. "For a minute there, you had me thinking you could actually handle the boys up in the Sabers front office."

"What makes you think I can't?"

"Sweetheart, those men would eat you alive in a contract negotiation. You don't know what hardball is until you go up against Milton Crawford and the rest of Sabers management. Besides—" he hefted the duffel bag's strap over his right shoulder "—there's a good reason I could never have you as my agent."

"And what's that?" Payton inquired.

With a wicked grin tipping up the corner of his mouth, his eyes made another journey down her body, hovering at breast level before climbing back to her face. "I'd spend every minute we're together picturing you naked."

He winked, turned and left her standing in the middle of the locker room.

"How can you say I'm difficult to work with, Powers? We've never worked together."

"Stop moving," came another frustrated reprimand above his shoulder.

Cedric raised his head from the massage table's cushioned face cradle and mouthed *sorry* to the trainer who'd been kneading the muscles in his upper back for the past half hour. Settling his face into the cradle, he adjusted the Bluetooth device in his ear and returned his focus to Aiden Powers, agent to his former teammate Thelonious Stokes. Powers was the fifth agent Cedric had talked to this week, and from the way this conversation was going, he was about to get another "I'll have to think about it."

And that would be the good scenario. He'd had three agents tell him flat-out no.

"You'd be crazy not to take me on," Cedric continued. "Didn't you see that thirty-two-yard touchdown run today? I'm money in the bank."

"Not as much as you could be. After the stunt you pulled at the Baltimore game, Reliant Sportswear backed out of the deal they were about to offer you."

How did Powers know about the Reliant thing?

Cedric had just gotten word that the deal was off two days ago. No doubt Gus had been flapping his gums. He should have known agents gossiped like a bunch of girls.

"That incident in Baltimore was a big misunderstanding. Watch the tapes. You'll see it was one of the fans who started it by throwing that bottle onto the field. The commissioner is even thinking about revoking the fine the league charged me. Reliant is going to come crawling back when that happens. You'll see. I've got—"

The high-powered agent cut him off. "Look, I don't have time for this, Cedric. You lost Reliant, you've pissed off Sabers upper management more times than I can count—face it, Milton Crawford has never liked you being on his team."

"What are you talking about? Crawford loves me," he said, referring to the owner of the Sabers. Sure, the big man had called him out a few times, but that was nearly four years ago, during his rookie season. It was all water under the bridge.

"No, he doesn't." Powers's reply was dry and matter-of-fact. "But that doesn't matter. As long as you perform on the field, Crawford will tolerate you. It's the other stuff. You're banned from most of the nightclubs in New York!"

"Only two clubs and neither incident was my fault," Cedric defended himself. "They were both a matter of me being in the wrong place at the wrong time."

"That's the problem. Being in the wrong place at the wrong time seems to be standard operating procedure for you. You're a magnet for trouble. A loose cannon. Even if you were able to get a deal with Reliant Sportswear, it wouldn't be enough commission for the headache you would cause. Try calling Sammy Hester. I heard he just lost the Tennessee quarterback to David Sage. He's probably looking for fresh meat."

"I don't trust Sammy Hester," Cedric said. Besides, Hester had turned him down when Cedric had called him on Thursday. "I need you, Powers. That deal you landed for Theo with Sports Talk TV was sweet. I need someone like you in there when the Sabers renegotiate my deal at the end of the season."

There was a pause on the other end of the phone. "Reeves," the agent said, weariness in his voice. "I'm going to tell you something you probably haven't accepted yet, but you need to face it. Despite that nice run you had today, the likelihood that the Sabers will renew your contract is slim. Have you been watching any football on Saturdays? 'Bama, Nebraska, USC and Georgia Tech all have running backs that are just as good as you are, and from what I know of them, they're not likely to get thrown out of nightclubs on a weekly basis.

"The league is cleaning up its image, and guys like you are becoming too much of a liability. Teams would rather take a chance on new talent than to sign a known troublemaker."

Cedric shut his eyes, the effects of a half hour on the massage table evaporating with that one word.

Troublemaker.

He hated that damn label, but once you were painted a certain color it was hell to wash yourself clean of it. Yeah, he'd made some knuckleheaded moves in the past, but he wasn't some hotheaded rookie anymore. Why couldn't anyone see that?

"I'll be straight with you, Powers. I need an agent.

A good agent. This is my first contract renegotiation. I need someone who knows what they're doing."

Aiden Powers's sigh came through loud and clear over the Bluetooth. "I would tell you that I'd think about it, but it would be a waste of your time, Reeves. My answer is no. I've got a full slate of clients, and even though they all may not be choirboys, I don't have to worry about picking them up from the local precinct at three in the morning, either."

Cedric winced at the reminder. Powers hadn't gotten that tidbit from hanging around the agent watercooler. News of his near arrest had been in every major newspaper and on every sports blog in the country. Another case of his being at the wrong place at the wrong time, but the reporters didn't bother themselves with reporting the whole story, only the stuff that fed his bad-boy image. Cedric was getting damn tired of that image.

"Good luck finding someone," Powers said before disconnecting.

Cedric's head sunk deeper into the massage table's face cradle, disappointment attacking him like a quarter-back blitz. Aiden Powers hadn't been his last hope, but he was close to it.

When his former agent had told him he was dropping him as a client, Cedric hadn't imagined he'd have trouble finding another one. He'd won the Doak Walker Award for top running back in the nation his senior year at Penn State and had been in contention for Rookie of the Year his first year in the league. He was one of the top running backs in the entire NFL, dammit. What agent wouldn't want to represent him?

Those who didn't want to be saddled with a trouble-maker.

"Cedric, you've got to relax, man. Your deltoids feel like speed bumps. There's only so much my magic fingers can do."

Cedric raised his head and looked up at Tony, one of the trainers who worked with the Sabers running core. "Thanks for trying, but I'm too stressed to relax," he answered.

"There's only one other thing I can think of that'll relieve the stress, but I can't help you with that one. Maybe some of the Saberrettes are still around."

Cedric chuckled as he levered himself off the massage table. "The Saberrettes are off-limits," he said, referring to the Sabers cheerleading squad. "Haven't you heard it's dangerous to play around in the workplace?"

"Not like I'd have the chance," Tony said with a hint of bitterness as he wiped massage oil from his fingers. "They won't even look at us guys not wearing football uniforms."

"From what I've heard from a couple of the guys on the team, you're not missing much. Hey, thanks for the work on my back," Cedric offered as he tucked the towel around his waist. "I may try soaking in the hot tub at home. See if that helps."

"Good idea," Tony said. "Hey, Reeves. Sorry about the whole thing happening with your agent." Tony gestured to the Bluetooth attached to Cedric's ear. "I couldn't help but hear, you know?"

He shrugged. "There are more agents out there than ball players. I'm just being choosy." Cedric pointed a finger at the massage table. "Tomorrow? Same time, same place?" Maybe the consecutive massages would make a dent in the weight he carried on his shoulders.

Cedric grabbed the duffel bag he'd stored underneath the table and retrieved the clothes he'd stripped out of before his massage. A metallic silver business card fell to the floor. Cedric scooped it up and turned it over.

"Mosely Sports Management. Payton Mosely, Owner."

He recognized the email address as the one that had cluttered his in-box.

Cedric shook his head and chuckled as he tossed the business card into his bag. When had she even managed to slip that in there? Ms. Mosely went after what she wanted, he'd give her that. He wondered if she was a Ms. or a Mrs. If he didn't have so much on his plate these days, he would take the time to find out. Images of that pretty face and those fantastic breasts had been hovering at the edge of his mind since their encounter in the locker room.

Cedric dropped the towel from his waist and pulled on his black sweatpants and black Sabers T-shirt. He made his way over to the suite of offices and conference rooms where postgame meetings were held. Personnel were filing out of the wrap-up meeting for the offense coaches. Cedric signaled to the Sabers's wide-receivers coach, Torrian Smallwood, as he exited the conference room.

Torrian had been sidelined by an eye disease that had left his vision too messed up to play but plenty good enough to coach. This was his first season coaching the Sabers wide-receiver core.

They clasped palms. "Nice run for that touchdown. You had the closest man beat by five yards."

"I had the wind at my back," Cedric joked.

"Whatever, man. It put us back in the game."

"What time are we meeting?" Cedric asked him. For the past few years, Cedric, Torrian, Theo Stokes and his fellow teammate Jared Dawson had met in Torrian's rec room after home games for dominoes, junk food and beer.

"You didn't get my text message?" Torrian asked. "Paige scheduled some big-time food critic to eat at the Fire Starter Grille tonight. I've got to be there. Plus Theo's plane was delayed by storms in the Midwest. He's still stuck in Omaha."

"I caught a bit of the Nebraska game last night. Theo's doing a good job as sideline commentator." Something Aiden Powers had said to him sounded a bell in Cedric's brain. "That running back at Nebraska looked pretty sharp. You know if the boys in the front office are looking at him?"

"I've heard his name mentioned," Torrian replied. His ex-teammate leveled him with a stare. "It's not time to start worrying about your job yet, Cedric. Just keep having games like the one you had today and keep your behind out of trouble. In fact, why don't you come by the restaurant tonight?"

"Nah, I'm good, Wood," he said, calling Torrian by his nickname. "I need to go through a few routes in the playbook."

"You'll be here tomorrow watching tape?"

"Probably get in around eleven."

"See you then. Good game, man." Torrian brought him in for a one-armed hug, then continued down the corridor.

Cedric gripped the handles of his duffel and made his way out to the parking lot. His stride faltered when he noticed the slim figure leaning against the concrete pillar a few spots down from where he'd parked his Lincoln Navigator. She straightened when she spotted him walking toward her.

"Hello again, Ms. Mosely," Cedric greeted her with

exasperation. "You sure you don't have anything better to do on a Sunday afternoon? Hanging around a parking lot isn't all that exciting."

"All I want is twenty minutes," she said.

"And just what is it you think you can accomplish in twenty minutes?"

"I can show you just what I can do for you," she answered.

Cedric's eyes zeroed in on her lips. They looked so inviting, so extremely kissable. Could they really be as soft as they appeared?

Cedric gave himself a mental shake and got back to the matter at hand. "Look here, sweetheart—"

"It's Payton."

"Fine, *Payton*. I appreciate a woman who goes after what she wants—"

She held up a hand, cutting him off. "First, try not to see me as a woman, since that's obviously one of your hang-ups."

Cedric dragged his gaze over her well-put-together body. "Baby, there's no other way to see you."

Every single inch of her was woman, from the silky hair that fell just above her shoulders to her delicate white-tipped toenails. Her dark denim jacket accentuated firm, round breasts and a tiny waist. Her skirt hit just above her knee, leaving her sexy, caramel-colored legs bare.

All woman, indeed.

"If we're going to work together, you're going to have to lay off the innuendoes," she informed him. "I expect you to treat this relationship as professionally as you would if you were working with a male agent."

"First, we're not going to work together. Secondly, should I remind you that *you're* the one who's been stalking *me?* It's pretty bold of you to start laying down rules when you're the one who's in need here."

"How many agents have you contacted within the past week, Mr. Reeves?"

"It's Cedric," he said. "If I'm going to call you Payton for the next—" he glanced at his watch "—five minutes I plan to entertain you, we might as well be on a level playing field, right?"

She folded her arms across her chest. "You didn't answer my question."

"Sorry, got distracted," Cedric said, looking pointedly at her breasts that were made more pronounced by her posture. She quickly dropped her arms. Cedric grinned.

"Why don't you stop dodging my question? How many agents have you spoken to this week?" she asked again.

"A few," he answered, enjoying this probably more than he should.

"Any of them talk to you longer than five minutes?"

Cedric switched his duffel from one hand to the other. Her gibe had hit its mark, and he suddenly wasn't enjoying her company so much.

"Face it, Cedric. You can't afford to just write me off. Not without at least hearing what I can offer. You'd be a fool to let some sexist notion that women can't be sports agents get in your way."

"Believe it or not, the fact that you're a woman has nothing to do with why I don't want you as my agent." Her brows rose. "It's because you don't have a single client," Cedric continued. "I need someone with experience."

"I may not have much experience—"

"No experience," Cedric interjected.

"I have a Jurist Doctor and chaired the Texas State Bar's committee on sports and entertainment law. I was one of the top associates in my law firm's contracts and negotiations division, and I can promise that I know this game better than half of your Sabers teammates." She pulled at the hem of her jacket, straightening it. "All I'm asking for is twenty minutes. You owe me that much for ogling my breasts."

Cedric barked out a laugh. What the hell? He'd had a good game today. Why not reward himself with an afternoon in the company of a gorgeous woman? "Fine," he finally relented. "There's a Starbucks about two blocks from here."

"I know where it is," Payton said. "Are you going there now?"

"As soon as you stop blocking the way to my truck."

She moved out of the way, but before Cedric could take a step toward his vehicle she caught him by the arm, halting him. "I expect to see you there in ten minutes."

Cedric looked down at the fingers nestled against his black shirt. He could feel the power in them. There was something about a petite, delicate-looking woman hiding that kind of strength that turned him on.

His gaze trailed from where she touched his arm to her warm brown eyes. The current of electricity that traveled between them was hot enough to singe his skin.

"I'll be there," Cedric promised.

Her fingers remained on his arm several seconds longer than necessary before she seemed to snap out of the lust-filled snare that had trapped them. She released his arm and inclined her head with a firm nod before heading in the direction of the visitors parking lot.

As he watched her walk away, Cedric wondered if he would be able to last the twenty minutes he'd promised her without thinking about how the rest of her looked beneath that denim jacket.

## Chapter 2

Payton added a packet of raw cane sugar to her black coffee and took a sip. She stared at the entrance to the coffee shop, her anxiety building with every nanosecond that passed. Cedric couldn't have been more than five minutes behind her, unless someone had detained him in the parking lot after she'd left. Or maybe he had stood her up despite his promise not to.

Payton had known this wouldn't be easy. From the moment she'd left her position at one of the most prestigious law firms in Austin and boarded a plane for New York, Payton had anticipated the series of brick walls she'd come up against with frustrating regularity.

It didn't matter how hard it was to break into the business, she reminded herself. As long as it kept her close to her dad.

Some of her earliest memories were of being on her

daddy's shoulders as he bellowed at his players from the sidelines of the Manchac High School Mustangs football practices. From the age of two until high school graduation, Payton had attended nearly every practice, coaches meeting and Friday night game. She understood the ins and outs of the West Coast Offense, and how to defend against it. She could draw up pass routes, devise a running play and figure out an opposing team's defense strategy as soon as they stepped up to the line of scrimmage.

But she had ovaries and thus couldn't possibly be a legitimate agent in the NFL.

Payton squelched her frustration. She'd expended enough energy debating this argument in her head.

She checked the time on her cell phone again. When she looked up she found Cedric holding the door open for a young couple who were exiting the coffee shop. Relief flowed over her at the sight of him. He hadn't backed out on her. This was further than she'd ever been able to get before with a potential client.

He pointed to a table in the rear of the coffee shop. Payton met him there.

"Sorry for making you wait. I had an important call I needed to take." He set the leather-bound notebook he'd carried in with him on the table. It had the Sabers logo embroidered on the cover, a growling saber-toothed tiger.

"That's okay. I knew you would be here," she lied.

He gestured to her cup. "You want a pastry with that?"

"No, thanks," Payton said.

He walked to the counter without as much fanfare as Payton would have expected. With its close proximity to the stadium, the regulars were probably used to seeing Sabers players in their local coffee shop. Several of the customers in line congratulated Cedric on his touchdown, but there was no fawning. Payton noticed he declined when a couple of people tried to let him skip the line.

As she waited, she peeked at the notebook he'd left on the table. Payton instantly recognized the scrawled drawings as football plays. A genuine NFL playbook. What her daddy wouldn't have given to have had a chance to thumb through this. She perused several of the plays, agreeing with some, finding flaws in others.

"That's confidential," Cedric said with a hint of a smile as he returned to the table.

"Then you probably shouldn't leave it just lying around," Payton quipped.

"I trust the guys who hang out here. I just have to watch out for the occasional Giants fan lurking around, trying to catch a glimpse of the playbook."

She trailed her fingers across the smooth leather. "Pretty interesting reading."

"Yeah, I'm sure it would keep you fascinated for hours," he snorted.

"Actually, it would," Payton replied. "Though some of those plays could use a bit of tweaking."

His brow cocked in surprise. "Do tell."

She pointed to the most obvious. "As soon as you line up in a T formation the defense expects you to run to the right. It would be smarter to bring in someone else as an eligible running back, to trip them up. Or maybe even run a reverse."

His eyes darted to the playbook then back to hers. He turned the notebook and studied the play.

"How'd you come up with that?" he blurted, clearly impressed.

"I told you, I know football." It was time for her to make her pitch. Payton didn't want to waste any more of her twenty minutes. "I also know how valuable you are to the Sabers running game, even if front-office management doesn't."

"Really?" He leaned back and folded his arms across his chest. "What do you know?"

"I know it would be a mistake for them to go with another running back at this stage of Mark Landon's career," she said, referring to the Sabers starting quarterback who'd announced plans to retire at the end of next season.

"And how would you convince Sabers management that Landon's retirement has anything to do with me?"

"Mark Landon has been handing you the ball for the past four years. When players work that closely together for an extended period of time, they develop a natural rhythm. If management brought in a new running back, that chemistry would be lost. Landon and the new guy would have to learn each other's nuances. Then, one season later, a new quarterback would have to go through the same learning process. Whereas if they stuck with you, they could bring in Landon's replacement early and get a head start on the grooming process between the two of you."

Payton hadn't realized she'd been leaning in as she spoke. She was halfway across the table by the time she finished. She couldn't help it; football talk excited her. Payton sat back in her chair and folded her hands on the table, trying her best to rein in her enthusiasm.

"That's just one of the reasons the Sabers should sign you to a new contract," she said much more calmly.

"By the time we go in for negotiations, I'll have enough reasons to fill that entire playbook."

"Damn." Cedric laughed. "Even I wasn't that sure the Sabers should re-sign me." He eyed her over the rim of his coffee cup. "How many other players have underestimated you?" he asked.

"Enough," Payton answered.

He took another sip of his coffee, set the cup on the table and raised his arms above his head in a huge stretch. "It's their loss," he replied.

Payton's breath seized in her lungs. Was he saying what she thought he was saying?

"Before I agree to let you represent me, you've got to answer a few questions."

"Shoot," she said, the blood pumping through her veins like a racehorse at the Kentucky Derby.

"How many times did you take the Players Association's certification test before you passed?"

"Once."

"Money. What's your cut?"

"The standard four percent for the contract, twenty percent for endorsement deals. Anything else?" she asked.

"Yeah." Cedric settled his elbows on the table. "How in the hell does an itty-bitty thing like you know so much about football?"

"Looks can be very deceiving, Mr. Reeves."

"Apparently. You had me fooled up until the point you revamped one of our best running plays and made it ten times better. How'd you manage to do that?"

"I'm a huge fan," she said with a shrug.

"That stadium was filled with over seventy-thousand fans today, and I'll bet half of them couldn't even read this playbook. You didn't learn how to dissect that play just by being a fan."

"My dad coached high school football," Payton shared. "While most families discussed current events at the dinner table, we talked end around plays and pass routes." She hitched a shoulder. "It's what I'm used to."

"I'll be damned," Cedric said, a rueful gleam in his eyes. "How many times did I blow you off?"

"More times than I can count."

"I'm lucky you're so persistent."

"I had to be," Payton said. "You're the player I need."

That brow hitched again. "How did I win that honor?"

"Because you're the one who will be the most difficult to get signed to a new contract."

His forehead creased in a frown, but Payton couldn't be bothered by hurt feelings. This was business, plain and simple.

"You're a hard sell, Cedric. You haven't made the best name for yourself these past few years. If I manage to get you a new contract, other players in the league would have no choice but to see me as a legitimate agent."

Instead of protesting, as Payton thought he would, he nodded and leaned both arms on the table. "Smart strategy," he commented. "So, how do you plan to convince the Sabers to re-sign me?"

"Are you agreeing to become my client?" she asked, reminding herself to take a breath but unable to get air past the lump in her throat. His answer meant everything to her career.

"As much as I wish it weren't true, I don't have much of a choice," he admitted. "Though you probably knew that already. These past few weeks I've discovered just how much agents talk."

"For obvious reasons, I'm not allowed membership into their special club, so I'm not privy to all the insider information," Payton said. "But your agent troubles aren't all that private. It's pretty much common knowledge."

With a disgruntled moan, he shook his head. Payton reached over and put a hand on his arm. His eyes met and held her gaze for several moments before she had the good sense to take her hand away.

"Don't worry," Payton said, resisting the urge to rub her palm where she'd touched him. Who knew a simple touch could have such an effect on her? "Everything people know about Cedric Reeves is about to change."

"How's that?" he asked.

"Because the first step in my plan is a complete reputation overhaul. You, Mr. Reeves, are about to go from bad boy to Boy Scout."

A dozen protests sounded throughout Cedric's brain, warning him this was a mistake. He didn't know anything about this woman, other than that she had great legs, serious skills as a stalker and apparently *did* know the game of football better than half the players on the Sabers team.

But could he trust her with his career?

Cedric glanced over at the counter where she'd gone to refill her coffee. She seemed legit and she talked a really good game. Wasn't that what he needed in an agent? Someone who knew how to say all the right words to convince the Sabers that they needed him?

"What do I know?" Cedric murmured under his breath as he ran an agitated hand down his face.

The guys had tried to tell him that he needed to pay attention to the business side of this league, but that's what Gus was for. From the day he'd approached Cedric during his sophomore year at Penn State, Gus Houseman had promised to take care of him. And he had. Gus had given him a generous—albeit illegal—monthly stipend throughout his college career, and on NFL Draft Day it was Gus who had treated Cedric's entire family to a huge barbecue back in Philadelphia while Cedric and his mom lived it up in New York where the draft was held. An investment, Gus had called it.

But those days were behind him. Gus had cut him loose, leaving Cedric when he was most vulnerable, in the middle of the season before his contract came up for renegotiation.

His mom always told him the only person who would ever really take care of him was himself. He should have listened.

His agent troubles were real. It had taken several weeks of rejections by big-name agents for Cedric to finally see the light, but he saw it now, shining brighter than the halogen bulbs that lit up Sabers Stadium. If the Sabers didn't re-sign him, there was no guarantee another team would pick him up. Cedric had never allowed himself to even contemplate that he would ever be one of those highly touted college players who washed out of the league after only a few years.

He wasn't here just for himself. He had his twin brother to think about. A half hour ago, just as Cedric was preparing to leave Sabers Stadium, Derek had made his weekly call from Marshall's Place, the top-notch facility for cerebral palsy patients Cedric gladly paid a small fortune to every month. His brother's care had no price tag. And his brother's love for football had no bounds. When he'd been drafted into the NFL, Cedric knew he was playing for both of them. He refused to crush Derek's dreams, which is why he had to stay in the league for as long as possible.

A running back's career was one of the shortest in the NFL; it had to be. No matter how much conditioning it went through, there was only so much the human body could endure. But his body still had years to give to this game. Not playing wasn't an option.

Payton resumed her seat on the other side of the table, clutching another cup of steaming coffee. Cedric couldn't help but notice how smooth her skin looked. *Focus,* he chastised himself, but it was damn hard to do when faced with a woman who looked like an angel and had the body of a swimsuit model. God, what he wouldn't give to see her in a swimsuit. Or, even better, out of one.

Cedric squelched a groan.

"So, do we have a deal?" she asked.

He snapped out of his daze, her question reminding him of just why they were sitting here. "You still haven't told me how it is you plan to score me a new contract."

"Yes, I did. You're going to have an image make-over."

"What does that entail, exactly?"

"Making sure the only section of the paper your face is seen is the sports section. Putting an end to those drama-filled extracurricular activities you seem so fond of. In other words, you, Cedric Reeves, have got to become the model NFL player both on and off the field.

"There are twelve regular games left in this season, which is more than enough to prove yourself on the field. We get a little more time to work on your off-the-field image, since negotiations won't take place until the off-season."

"And you think that's enough time to turn things around?"

"Only if you stick with the plan," she said.

"And that plan?"

"Is well thought out and ready to be put into motion. But you've got to sign on the dotted line first."

"What?" Cedric laughed. "You expect me to take you on as my agent without knowing what it is you plan to do for me? You think I'm stupid or something?"

"Do you think *I'm* stupid?" she returned. "Am I supposed to just hand over this strategy I've devised so you can take it to some other, more 'experienced' agent, who just so happens to have testicles? I was born in the summer of seventy-nine, Cedric, not yesterday."

She sipped her coffee, sat back in her chair and lanced him with a piercing stare. "I know how female agents are viewed in this league," she continued. "You all think just because a woman can't play football, she couldn't possibly understand the game enough to be a competent agent."

"You've already proven that you know football," Cedric said.

"To you, but what about to your teammates? And all those reporters who cover the Sabers games? The moment they find out I'm your new agent they're going to rag on you like a bunch of kids on a playground, but you've got to promise that you'll stand up to the criticism. If we become partners, you've got to show them you're serious about me, Cedric. No cute jokes about the girl agent. Are we clear on that?"

Any inclination to make a joke about her being female had been washed away by another, stronger inclination. Though it, too, had everything to do with her being female. The color in her smooth brown cheeks had heightened and her chest rose and fell with her escalated breaths. Cedric reined in the urge to reach across the table and tuck back the strand of hair that had gone astray during her impassioned speech.

"So, do we have a deal?" Payton asked.

She unclasped the black handbag she'd hung on the back of the chair and retrieved a tri-folded sheaf of papers. She unfolded what Cedric realized was a contract. The woman came prepared.

"This contract states that you agree to be represented by Mosely Sports Management for the rest of this football season, including the free-agency period. At the end of that time, if either of us is dissatisfied with the relationship, we can end it." She held out a pen. "This season, Cedric. Give me this one season to turn your career around. I promise you won't be sorry."

Cedric stared at her across the table. His brain told him to take the contract back to his place, read it, think it over. Then, after careful deliberation, make his decision.

But his gut told him Payton Mosely was the real deal. And it wasn't as if he had agents lined up at the door, begging to represent him. He was about to move to his C-list, and in the span of a half hour Payton had impressed him more than any of those guys. Hell, she was sharper than half the agents on his B-list. Her lack of experience was the only knock against her, but every agent had to start somewhere. He could either throw caution to the wind and become her guinea pig or walk away and hope he could convince another agent to sign him.

Forget that. Why should he go begging for their scraps? Payton was ready to take a chance on him. It was only right that he return the favor.

Relying on his gut instinct that told him Payton Mosely was legit, Cedric picked up the pen she'd placed on the table and flipped to the last page of the three-page contract. He scrawled his signature on the line above his typed name.

"When do we start making me into the new Cedric Reeves?"

# Chapter 3

Payton stood against the back wall of the press room, her nerves in knots. Dave Foster, the head coach of the Sabers, was still fielding endless questions from reporters. He sat at a table centered on a three-foot-high platform, the wall behind him speckled with pictures of the Sabers roaring mascot.

Cedric would be out here any minute, sitting at the same table, answering some of the same questions. But Payton knew there would be an additional question for Cedric, one the reporters had asked him at every postgame press conference since he'd been released from Gus Houseman's client roster. This time, Cedric would have a different answer for them.

She and Cedric had decided to wait until the Sunday postgame interviews to announce their new partnership. The way Payton saw it, today was the beginning of the career she'd dreamed of for so long. She had spent the entire week fine-tuning her strategy for the next three months. She had Cedric's schedule detailed to the very minute. The busier she kept him, the less likely he was to find himself in some sort of trouble.

The Sabers head coach answered one last question. A minute later, Cedric, along with fellow running back Thomas Grayson, sat before the microphones at the table the coach had just vacated.

His eyes locked with hers and a jolt of sensation shot through Payton's body. It was that feeling she got whenever he was near. It made her skin tingle and her stomach knot with a desire that threatened her quest to remain professional around him. His mouth tipped up in a secret grin that Payton was too nervous to interpret at the moment.

The thumping in her chest escalated with each question directed at Cedric. The one she'd been anticipating came from a reporter only a few feet away from her.

"Cedric, any luck with the agent hunt?" the reporter called.

"As a matter of fact, yes," he answered, straightening his shoulders and lifting his chin with such confidence, he had Payton thinking he meant it. "I've decided to sign with Mosely Sports Management."

There was a split second of silence, followed by a flurry of whispers and murmuring around the room. Finally, the reporter who had asked the initial question followed up with the query that was likely on the tip of everyone else's tongue. "Who?"

"My new agent is Payton Mosely, president of what will soon be the most sought-after outfit in professional sports management. She happens to be here today.

Payton?" He pointed to the back of the room and a hundred heads turned her way.

Payton nodded to the room of reporters and fought the urge to fidget. Instead, she took her cue from Cedric and straightened her shoulders and raised her chin a notch.

"Ms. Mosely and I have some exciting things planned. I'm looking forward to working with her," Cedric finished.

He lied with aplomb. He didn't know what she had planned, and Payton wasn't so sure he would be happy when he learned of what she had in store for him.

A man juggling a small voice recorder, camera and cell phone approached. "I'm Neil Cameron from *The Examiner*. Would you mind answering a few questions?"

"It would be my pleasure," she said.

Payton fed the reporter answers she'd already rehearsed to his very predictable questions. Why did you become a sports agent? Has it been hard breaking into the business as a woman?

The reporter switched the voice recorder to his other hand. "So, how did you land Cedric Reeves as a client?"

Payton wasn't prepared for *that* question. She still wasn't sure how she'd accomplished that feat.

"Persistence and keen negotiating skills," was her answer.

The reporter thanked her and turned his attention back to the front of the room, where two of the players who made up the Sabers defensive line—nicknamed the Wall of Destruction—had taken seats at the table.

"Hope you didn't mind my calling you out like that."

Payton jumped at Cedric's voice behind her. "No, of course not," she answered, turning to him. "Are you done here?"

"Until tomorrow when I have to be back to watch hours of tape."

"Are we meeting at the Starbucks again?" Payton asked.

"Would you mind coming over to my place?"

His request caught her off guard. "Uh, what's wrong with the Starbucks?"

Okay, so she could admit a coffee shop wasn't the most ideal place to conduct meetings, but she couldn't afford office space in New York for her one-woman operation. She could barely afford her seven-hundred-square-foot apartment in Weehawken, New Jersey.

But she wasn't sure she was comfortable enough with Cedric to be alone with him in his apartment. Though she wasn't certain who she had a harder time trusting, Cedric or herself.

God, she had to get past this insanely intense attraction. Her focus should be on landing her client a stellar deal, not on the way his uniform had outlined his sinewy thighs.

"I recorded today's game on my DVR," Cedric continued. "I want to get a jump start on analyzing my plays from today. I thought we could go over there, order takeout and go over things while I watch the game. I've got plans for later tonight so I need to get this done early."

His statement had the effect of a bucket of ice water being emptied over her head.

*Of course* he had plans for tonight. Tales of Cedric's play on the football field were trumped only by stories of his player status *off* the field. In the four years since he'd entered the league, he had been linked to at least a half-dozen starlets. How could she blame them? He was a young, rich, incredibly sexy football player. What woman wouldn't kill to be on his arm?

No, she didn't have to worry about Cedric ravishing her in his apartment; he probably had a dozen women lined up and all too willing to be ravished.

He produced a cell phone from his pocket. "You can follow in your car, but I'll text you my address just in case we get separated."

"Don't worry about it. I already know where you live."

He stopped with his fingers on the keys. "You do know stalking is a crime, right?"

Payton felt her cheeks heat. "I no longer have to stalk you, so why don't we just put that all behind us? Come on, I'll pick up some Chinese from that little place around the corner from your building."

His brows rose. "Do you know what my usual order is, too?"

"I hadn't gotten that far yet." Payton laughed.

Cedric had a condo in a high-rise steps away from the Hudson on Manhattan's west side. If she stood on the roof of her five-story walk-up across the river in Weehawken, she could see the last few floors of the sleek, fifty-plus-story ultramodern skyscraper where he lived.

As they pulled up to his block, her cell phone trilled on the seat next to her. Before she could utter a hello, Cedric said, "The code for the parking garage is one one seven five. My parking spots are on the third level, slots thirty-six and thirty-seven."

"What's your apartment number?"

"You mean you don't know it?"

Payton's eyes rolled at his sarcasm. "I may have stalked you a little but not to the extent you think. Sorry to bruise your ego, Mr. Reeves, but you're not all that."

His deep chuckle resonated through the phone. "As my agent, you're supposed to pump up my ego. Didn't they teach you that in agent school?"

"What's the apartment number?" Payton asked again.

He provided it as he turned into an entryway to an underground garage. The metal gate rose for him, then lowered seconds after he entered. Payton punched the code he'd given her into the keypad. When the gate rose, she saw Cedric's SUV waiting just inside the garage.

Her heart melted at his thoughtfulness.

"So he's hot and considerate. Get over it, he's a client," Payton said aloud. Her head whipped to the cell phone on her seat, her stomach tanking in the seconds before she saw that the phone was indeed off. If by some stupid technological glitch her phone had remained connected to Cedric's and he'd heard her muttered words, she would never have been able to face him.

Cedric pulled into a parking slot and Payton pulled in next to him.

She got out of her car and rounded it. Cedric was leaning into the back of his SUV. He came out with the alligator duffel bag that probably cost more than her entire wardrobe.

"What happened to my Chinese food?" Cedric asked. Payton winced. "I'm only teasing you," he continued with a chuckle. "I called in the order on our drive over. It'll be here any minute. Come on." He tipped his head toward the bank of elevators.

When the elevator doors closed, Payton said, "I'm trying to figure out if that's allowed."

"Chinese food?" Cedric asked, hefting the bag over his shoulder.

"No. Teasing."

"Last time I checked it wasn't against the law."

"We'll need to establish some boundaries, Cedric. I don't know how close you were with Gus Houseman—"

He cut her off. "There was no teasing with Gus."

"So there shouldn't be any with me."

He stared at her across the mirrored elevator, and the space seemed to shrink to half its size. He conceded with a simple nod. "Fine. This is a strictly professional partnership, right?"

"That's right," she declared, despite the voice in her head lobbying a protest against her words.

She ignored the confusing twinge of disappointment that edged along the perimeter of her brain. From the very beginning Payton realized that one of the most important things she would need to establish with her clients was boundaries. Being the ultimate football junkie, she knew she'd have to curb her fan-girl tendency of gushing over her favorite players. The fact that just being near Cedric sent her pulse into overdrive was even more reason to adhere to her vow to remain professional.

They took the parking garage elevators to the fifth floor, exited and slipped right into an open elevator directly across the hall. There were two people inside, who both immediately started hammering Cedric with questions about today's game. The elevator stopped several times to let residents on and off, then finally dinged its arrival at the thirty-eighth floor.

Cedric motioned for her to go first and then guided

her down the hallway. Payton tried not to gawk at the plush carpet that swallowed the heels of her simple black pumps, or the avant-garde artwork that decorated the soft gray walls.

Cedric opened the door to his unit and again motioned for her to go ahead of him. Payton's jaw dropped as soon as she entered the apartment. She quickly shut it but the astonishment remained as she took in the spectacular home before her.

The entryway was done in a beautiful cream-and-tan marble with streaks of bronze and gold swirling throughout. Payton followed Cedric from the marble dais, down three steps and into a spacious living area. The kitchen, den and bar were all part of one wide-open space done in the same understated cream and tan with splotches of dark brown, bronze and gold.

A doorbell sounded.

"That's probably the Chinese," Cedric said.

She went for her purse but Cedric stopped her. "I got this."

"I should pay."

He shook his head.

"At least let me cover my half," Payton argued.

"I'm going to eat way more than you will anyway," he said. "You can start picking up the tab once you land me a fat contract."

The doorbell rang again. Payton watched as Cedric stepped over to it and opened it for the delivery guy. She was uncomfortable with him paying for her dinner. It should be the other way around; she was the one still trying to woo him.

She walked over to the floor-to-ceiling windows that ran the length of the entire space. The corner apartment had one of the most amazing views Payton had ever seen.

In a slow span from right to left, she could see the Jersey end of the George Washington Bridge, along with the ridiculously high-priced condos along the Hudson, to the skyscrapers of downtown and midtown Manhattan.

"It's gorgeous at night," Cedric said, coming up behind her. She stiffened in shock at his undetected approach. "Last year, when the Sabers made it to the playoffs, the lights on the Empire State building were teal and white. I'd just sit here and stare at it for hours while running plays over and over in my head."

"This place really is incredible," Payton said, her eyes making another trip around the tastefully decorated space. She wasn't sure what she'd expected—mirrors on the ceiling, a stripper pole—but never such understated elegance.

"I like it," Cedric shrugged. "Pretty decent living for a kid from South Philly." His brow lifted in a wry arch. "It's up to you to make sure I keep it."

"You'll have to do your part," Payton said.

"I will," he stated with a seriousness Payton had yet to see in him up until this point. "It's been an eye-opening couple of weeks. I didn't think I'd be in this position after only four years in the league, but this is real. I'm putting a lot of faith in you, Payton. You've got to get me a new contract with the Sabers."

"I'm putting just as much faith in you. If I can't get you that contract, my career is over too. We're on the same team here, Cedric. We're going to need to work together. That's why when I lay out this plan I need your buy-in."

"Okay, then," he said. "Let's get started. Do we want to eat first?"

"We've got a lot to cover. I say we multitask."

They moved to the dining area that was tucked into

the corner of the den. Cedric picked up a remote control the size of a hardback novel and a flat-screen television that was no fewer than seventy-two-inches came to life. Cedric pressed a couple more buttons and commentators announced the start of the game Payton had just watched at Sabers Stadium between New York and Detroit.

"You won't have to watch the entire game," Cedric said. "I'll fast forward through the plays when Detroit is on offense."

"Except when their running back had that sixty-eight-yard run," Payton said, watching as the punter kicked the ball. "That spin move he made to get away from his defender was awesome. You should add it to your arsenal."

When Cedric didn't respond for several moments, she looked up to find him watching her with a curious smile.

"What?" Payton asked.

He shook his head. "I'm just not used to a woman who knows football so well. On the rare occasion I can get one to watch a game, I usually have to spend all my time explaining what's happening on the field. You are my kind of woman, Payton Mosely."

His words sent a tremor of desire cascading across her skin. The thought of being his kind of woman was all too enticing.

"So, are we going to work and eat?" she asked in an effort to remind herself that she was here in a professional capacity.

That smile at the edge of Cedric's mouth tipped up even more, but he didn't say another word, only nodded. Soon, the glass-topped table was covered with cartons of steaming noodles, beef and vegetables, sweet and sour chicken, spring rolls and stir-fried rice.

"This is enough food to feed a football team," Payton remarked.

"Or one very hungry football player," Cedric said, heaping rice onto his plate.

Payton passed on the wine he'd offered, sipping from a can of soda and loving every minute of it. Cedric didn't have diet and Payton had forgotten just how good a regular soda tasted.

"Okay," she said, unzipping the leather binder she'd brought in with her. "I took a two-way approach when coming up with this plan, for both on and off the field."

"I've got the on-the-field stuff covered."

"As far as executing plays," Payton said. "But you've got to work on your behavior on the field. Incidents like the one in Baltimore cannot happen again."

"That wasn't my fault," Cedric said. "One of the fans threw a bottle at me."

"Because you taunted them. You can't do that. Make your touchdown, celebrate with your teammates, then go back to the sideline. Leave the fans out of it, especially at hostile stadiums like Baltimore."

Slouched back in his seat, he twirled lo mein noodles around his fork. He glanced up at her. "I know it was stupid. I let my emotions get the better of me. I've been trying to work on that."

Sympathetic to the vulnerability she heard in his contrite tone, Payton nearly reached for his hand, but caught herself at the last minute and picked up a packet of soy sauce instead. His tone was likely to change with what she had to say next. Payton took a deep breath. This was the part she hadn't been looking forward to.

"As far as off the field, a whole lot will have to change."

"Like what? Wait." He held a hand up and raised the volume on the television. "Did you see how I got away from that middle linebacker? That was sweet."

"Yeah, but it would have been sweeter if you had cut to the right." She pointed at the TV with her chopsticks. "Look at the hole your offensive line made for you. The tackler wouldn't have taken you down if you'd run to the other side."

He used the remote to jump back a couple of frames and they watched the play again. "I'll be damned. Why didn't I see that?"

"Running backs tend to favor a certain side of the field," Payton said with a shrug. "Just remember to trust your offensive line. Those guys are there to protect you."

He shot her a smile. "You talk like a coach."

She couldn't help her own smile. "Thanks," she answered. "That's what I really wanted to do."

His brows peaked. "Coach?"

She nodded. "Just like my dad."

"He must be some kind of coach." Cedric laughed.

"He was," she answered. Payton pulled in a deep breath and held tears back by sheer will. "He died a little over a year ago. Heart attack, right in the middle of spring football practice."

Cedric sobered. "I'm sorry."

"If you're going to go, might as well go doing what you love, right?" she said, overly bright. She motioned toward the flat screen. "This was pretty hard to watch."

She and Cedric both winced as the Sabers quarterback threw his first of three interceptions.

"Let's get back to work," she said, turning back to

her Chinese, even though her appetite had exited stage left at the thought of her dad.

"Okay." Cedric bit into a spring roll, his appetite obviously still hard at work. "Off the field. What do you have in mind to turn me into the Dudley Do-Right of the league?"

Payton cut her eyes at him but didn't give him grief over his mocking. She shoved her plate to the side and opened the binder she'd brought in. "First things first," she stated. "Your entourage? They have to go."

"My what?"

"Your band of merry men who always seem to be around when there's trouble. Sound familiar?"

"I don't have an entourage. A few of the guys from my old neighborhood in Philly make the trip out here for a couple of games a season."

"Cedric, think back over the last four years. And if you can't remember that far, I've got proof here in black-and-white." She held up a copy of just one of several news stories she'd found online about Cedric's off-the-field shenanigans. "Every time there's been trouble, these guys have been there. They're not helping your image."

"But those guys *are* me," he insisted with an indignant frown. "I can't sell out just because I'm making a little money."

"Give me a break," Payton said with a disgusted snort. "I'm so tired of you professional athletes trying to cling to the same lifestyle you worked like crazy to leave behind. Look around you, Cedric. How many of your friends from back home live like this?"

Payton tried to infuse as much understanding in her voice as possible. "I know it seems as if you're turning your back on your past, but if your past is getting you into trouble, then it's time to let it go. They're no good for you, Cedric."

Instead of putting up the fight Payton had anticipated, he nodded and said, "I know. I've been feeling that way ever since they let me take the fall for the vandalism incident at that club on forty-fifth a few months ago. Mike and Damian were the ones who sprayed the place down with the fire extinguishers. I was on the other side of the club when it happened."

Cedric scrubbed a hand over his close-cut hair and let out a long sigh.

"I don't go searching for trouble," he continued. "I'm not trying to make excuses here, okay? I know I'm not a Boy Scout." He glanced at her with another one of those grins and winked. "At least not yet. But I'm not the bad boy the media has made me out to be, either. I've done some stupid things but they haven't all been my fault. It just seems as if the finger gets pointed at me whenever I'm around."

Payton shrugged. "You're an easy target."

His lips had thinned into a rigid line. Staring straight ahead, he said, "I'm tired of being the fall guy." He glanced over at her. "I guess it's time I start considering the consequences before I act, huh?"

"Yes," she said, relief washing over her at his willingness to be accountable for his behavior. "I know dropping your friends seems as if you're selling out—"

"It's not selling out." Cedric shook his head. "It's moving on."

Payton couldn't contain her smile. "And I've got the perfect new gang for you to hang out with," she said, sliding a homemade flyer from her binder.

"The Linden Avenue Recreation Center?" he asked

with a hint of incredulousness that caused Payton to grit her teeth.

"This one is a no-brainer. Everyone knows the quickest way to clean up a bad image is to start giving back to the community. I want you to hold some type of football thing at this rec center. You could get some of the other Sabers players to join in, and the mascot. Kids love mascots."

His eyes roamed over the flyer. "I don't know about this. It seems like a big time commitment."

Payton tried to keep the exasperation from her voice. "I'm not asking for you to recreate the Sabers off-season training camp, Cedric. I was thinking along the lines of a one-day event—a mini-football camp."

He mulled over the flyer for a few moments more, his expression hesitant. Tossing the flyer on the table, he said, "I'll consider the camp. I guess it wouldn't be that much of a hassle." He took a sip of his wine. "What else is on your list?"

"Second thing, endorsements."

"Now that's what I'm talking about," Cedric said. "Gus and I knocked heads when it came to endorsements. He never thought the time was right. Said I needed to wait until my breakout year."

"That's one strategy," Payton agreed. "But we don't have the luxury of waiting for your breakout year. This is it. We need to get you a deal."

"I want Reliant."

"You lost Reliant."

"I want them back."

"Cedric—"

"I'm willing to fight to get them back," he said.

"It isn't as easy as you think."

"I know that," he declared. "Gus wouldn't discuss endorsements. I'm the one who went after Reliant."

"You're also the one who lost them." He started to speak but Payton stopped him. "I'll see what I can do, but I can't make promises."

"Fine," Cedric relented. "So, we have the entourage, endorsements and giving back to the neighborhood. What else makes a model citizen in the NFL?"

Payton pointed to the television where Cedric was scrambling for what had turned into a forty-yard gain before being brought down at the Sabers five-yard line. On the next play, he'd run it in for a touchdown.

"You just continue to do that, Mr. Reeves, and we're in business."

# Chapter 4

"Is this all you've got, Stokes? I could have stayed home for this," Cedric said as he smacked another domino on the table.

"I called the Oregon game yesterday. My brain's still functioning on Pacific time," was Theo Stokes's excuse.

"Looks as if you left your game back on the West Coast along with your brain," Torrian muttered as he sipped from a longneck beer bottle.

Theo flipped off his old teammate, garnering chuckles from the table's other two occupants.

Cedric felt a certain comfort as he took in the guys seated around the gaming table in Torrian's basement. Even though two of them were no longer playing ball—Theo by choice and Torrian by necessity—whenever possible they still got together for dominoes, food and beer after Sabers home games.

Cedric was the motivation behind the ritual. After he'd pissed off the Sabers offensive line during his rookie season by suggesting they were playing for the opposing team, hanging out at the team's official postgame spot had become hazardous to his health. To keep Cedric out of trouble, Torrian had offered his home as an alternative.

Even though things had improved between Cedric and the rest of the team after that first season, no one wanted to give up the domino game. It had become somewhat of a postgame ritual.

The basement of Torrian's Manhattan brownstone was the ultimate Man Cave, equipped with a card table, pool table, several full-size arcade games and a gigantic flat-screen television. The rest of the Sabers could have their sports bar; this space, along with the guys who occupied it, was all Cedric needed.

Jared Dawson had joined them because he claimed he disliked crowds. Cedric had a feeling it was due to the under-the-table betting that went on at the bar. Jared's gambling issues were well-known around the Sabers locker room. If he were caught in anything that even seemed like gambling, Jared could kiss his NFL career goodbye.

"What's this?" Theo asked, picking up an oblong shaped hors d'oeuvre wrapped in bacon. Cedric had no idea what they were either, but those babies were off the chain. He'd eaten four already.

"It's a new appetizer Deirdre's trying out for the restaurant," Torrian answered. "Bacon-wrapped dates stuffed with parmesan cheese. You guys are supposed to let me know what you think."

Jared grabbed one and bit into it. "Not bad." He nodded, wiping his hands on his jeans.

Cedric reached over and snagged another from the tray that had been set up on the bar next to the game table. "I love being Deirdre's guinea pig," he said. "She needs to put together another dozen of these before I can give her a solid answer, though."

"I'll let her know that for next time." Torrian laughed. "She's not home tonight."

"I thought you said you'd hired another chef to oversee private events at the restaurant," Theo said, taking a sip of his beer.

"I didn't say she was at the restaurant," Torrian replied. "She's on a date."

Theo's head snapped up. "A *date?*"

"Yeah, a date," Torrian said.

"Go Deirdre." Cedric swigged his beer. "As long as this new guy doesn't stop her from cooking for us," he added.

Cedric noticed that Theo looked as if he were ready to throttle someone. Now *that* was interesting. He wasn't the most intuitive guy on the block, but when you played dominoes with a man every other Sunday, you picked up on stuff. He'd suspected Theo had had something for Torrian's sister.

"What about you?" It took Cedric a moment to realize Torrian's question had been directed toward him. "How are things working out with your new agent?"

Cedric shrugged. "As well as could be expected. We've only been working together about a week," he said. "Other than the obvious drawback, I guess she'll work out okay."

"What's the obvious drawback?" Jared smacked his domino on the table.

"If you say something about her not being able to do the job because she's a woman, I'll be forced to kick your butt on behalf of my soon-to-be fiancée," Torrian informed him.

Cedric rolled his eyes. "I'm not being sexist."

"Paige would beg to differ if she were here," Torrian said.

"I'm *not* being sexist," Cedric repeated. "Would you have been so quick to jump on David Sage's roster if he were a woman?"

"As long as he got me the deal I wanted," Torrian answered. With a grin he added, "It's so easy to be self-righteous when speaking in hypotheticals, isn't it?"

"Yeah, well, my agent trouble had moved way passed the hypothetical stage." Cedric hadn't shared the depth of his agent woes with his teammates. For a moment he debated whether he should say anything, but if Payton had been able to find out through the grapevine, he figured the talk would make its way to these guys soon enough. He'd rather they heard it from him.

"Nobody wanted me," Cedric admitted. "Payton was my only shot."

"Somebody would have taken you on, eventually," Jared said. "In the end it all comes down to dollars, and you're worth a lot of them."

"I don't blame you for not waiting for another agent to throw you a bone," Theo said. "Give Payton a chance. She may surprise you."

"She already has." Cedric recalled their earlier brainstorming session as they watched a replay of today's game. "She may not have much experience as an agent but she's sharp, and she knows football."

"She's also fine as hell," Jared commented.

"Hey, man, don't be looking at my agent like that."

"What? Everybody's looking at your agent like that. She's hot."

"How is she doing at her job?" Torrian interrupted, cutting his eyes at Jared. "You two working out okay?"

"We had our first official meeting today where she laid out her plans. My boys from Philly are out. She thinks they're no good for me."

"I could have told you that." Torrian snorted. "Those boys didn't have your back."

It took Payton pointing it out for Cedric to fully recognize that the guys from his old neighborhood were basically parasites. The only time they came around was when they needed something or wanted to party hard. They'd done nothing but mooch. Why had it taken him so long to see what was apparently clear to everyone else?

"She's also trying to put together a one-day mini-football camp for this community center up in Harlem the Saturday of our bye week," he said, referring to the weekend during the season when the team didn't play. "We can use a couple more players to help out."

"I'm in," Jared said. "Only other thing I have planned that weekend is Wood's engagement party."

"Paige and Deirdre are taking care of all of that stuff," Torrian said. "I have a few coaches meetings that morning, but I'll try to get out there for a little while and help out. This agent sounds good for you, man."

"I'm beginning to think she is." Cedric nodded.

"Is that all she is?" Jared asked. Cedric rolled his eyes. "Oh, come on, man. Don't give me that. You can't say you haven't thought about it."

What the hell did he think Cedric was? Blind? Dead? Of course he'd thought about it. He thought about it at least a thousand times a day. Sometimes, when they were together, it took all he had to concentrate on the words

Payton was saying instead of the way her lips formed around them. God, her mouth was sexy. Everything about her was sexy.

For the past week, whenever he closed his eyes at night, Payton appeared, dressed in that slim skirt and a white shirt with the buttons undone down to her navel. She'd strut toward him in slow motion, her eyes smoldering with the same fiery desire that raced through his veins.

Then the team would douse him with a jug of icy Gatorade.

He'd been tortured by the wet-dream-turned-nightmare since last Sunday, the day Payton had conned her way into the Sabers locker room and flipped his world on its side. He had to get a handle on this fascination with her before it ruled him more than it already did.

Payton had laid the ground rules. Everything between them was to be kept at a purely professional level. His brain knew this, but every other part of his body was clamoring for more.

"Sounds as if Payton is more of a go-getter than Gus Houseman was," Torrian said.

Cedric shrugged off the hit against his former agent. "Gus didn't have the incentive to do any more for me than what he was doing. He has a roster full of players. The way I see it, Payton has just as much at stake here as I do. I'm her only client. If she doesn't get me a deal at the end of the season, she may not get any more players to sign with her. She's going to work hard to make sure that doesn't happen."

"Listen to you, talking like you know about the business side of this stuff," Jared joked.

It was Cedric's turn to flip his teammate the bird.

"It's about time you started to take this seriously," Torrian said. "I've been telling you guys you've got to be concerned about more than just what's happening on the field. There's gonna come a time when you're not on the field anymore, and you never know when that's gonna happen."

Theo, who had been studying his dominoes as if they held clues to the meaning of life, popped his head up and turned toward the stairs. "Was that the door?" he asked.

"The door? Man, what's up with you?" Cedric asked Theo, who'd been silent through much of the conversation.

"Huh?" Theo shook his head. "Hey, are we done here?" He let the dominoes fall to the table as he rose from his seat. "I forgot I had something to do tonight."

"We're in the middle of a game," Jared argued.

"We'll finish it next Sunday," Theo returned.

"We have an away game next week," Cedric reminded him.

"Then just finish without me," Theo said, shoving his arms into his leather coat.

Cedric glanced at Torrian, who had yet to voice a protest at their prematurely aborted game. Torrian balanced his chair on the two back legs and grinned at Theo.

"Kick some Cardinal ass next week in Arizona," Theo said as he jogged up the stairs.

They all just stared at the empty stairway leading up to Torrian's first floor.

"What was that about?" Jared finally asked.

Torrian shook his head. "I think Theo needs to figure it out for himself."

Cedric turned to him. "Have you been hanging out with Obi-Wan Kenobi? Chill out with all this 'enlightened one' crap. It's starting to freak me out."

"Shut up," Torrian drawled. He pushed his dominoes away and nodded toward the pool table. "Playtime's over. Grab a cue stick. It's time for me to school you two."

Cedric and Jared glanced at each other and nodded. Then they both tackled Torrian to the floor.

Checking his rearview mirror, Cedric noticed the sun just beginning to rise as he took the exit ramp from I-95. He'd finally discovered the secret to avoiding traffic on this oft-repeated trip: hit the Jersey Turnpike just a few minutes before six a.m. The drive from Manhattan to Woodbridge, New Jersey, had taken him just over an hour. Not bad considering it usually took him two hours to get to the group home where his brother resided.

Cedric meandered his way through Woodbridge Township, taking in the peacefulness at dawn. At seven a.m. on a Monday morning there would be a sea of humanity clogging the sidewalks of Manhattan, but other than a couple of joggers and the occasional businessman walking to his office, Woodbridge residents were still easing into their weekday.

He turned into the parking lot of Marshall's Place. Yesterday, when he'd made his weekly postgame call to his brother, he'd asked Mrs. Bea, the group home's director, whether he could come in early this morning to see Derek. His upcoming schedule would prevent Cedric from seeing his twin for at least a month.

When Cedric walked to the steps of the home for the mentally and physically handicapped—which really was a *home,* not some sterile institution—Mrs. Bea was waiting for him on the porch. Marshall's Place was named for her own son who'd died of complications from cerebral palsy. She took care of the patients in this home as if they were her own flesh and blood. The small, unassuming facility was touted as the best care center for cerebral palsy patients in the country.

Cedric had given the press a dozen reasons why he wanted to spend his entire career with the Sabers, but no one knew the one true reason he wanted to remain in New York. Marshall's Place was the ultimate in caring for patients with Derek's condition, and the New York Sabers were the closest NFL franchise to Woodbridge, New Jersey.

Cedric *had* to remain a New York Saber. There was no other option.

"Good morning," Mrs. Bea greeted him from the porch of the group home.

"Morning, Mrs. Bea. Thanks for letting me come in so early."

"You are welcome at any time, Cedric. There is nothing that lights up Derek's face more than when he sees you, either in person or on the screen."

"Did he make everyone in the house watch yesterday's game?"

"Of course." Mrs. Bea nodded. "That's okay. I've got a home filled with Sabers fans."

Cedric held the screen door open for her before following her into the large house that had been renovated to accommodate both kids and adults with special needs. Cedric had personally funded several of the renovations himself.

"Your mother drove up from Philadelphia yesterday," the director commented in a lowered voice as they made their way through the house.

"I know. I was hoping she would stay an extra night, but she had to get back to work. She thinks the elementary school will fall apart without its principal."

"She's very dedicated to her students, and to Derek, too. You should have seen him preening as she cheered him on yesterday during his lessons."

"So he's doing better?" Cedric asked.

"Much better," Mrs. Bea answered. "He's been getting less frustrated with his lessons, and the new hydrotherapy sessions are really helping with his motor skills. I think you'll be surprised when you see him." She motioned for Cedric to follow her. "He's already dressed and waiting in the sunroom. I wanted your visit to be a surprise, so I told him he was going into the pool early this morning."

Mrs. Bea guided Cedric past the kitchen and down the hallway, where the extra-wide, wheelchair-friendly bedroom doors were still closed. They made a quick left into the sunroom, and Cedric spotted his brother looking out into the vast backyard.

"Derek," Mrs. Bea called. "There's someone here to see you."

Derek turned his head and his eyes opened wide as saucers.

"Cedric!"

"What's up, buddy?" Cedric greeted, stooping so he could capture his twin in a bear hug. Cedric swallowed past the lump that always formed in his throat whenever he encountered his brother's unrestrained love.

Derek worshipped him, which only made Cedric's guilt that much harder to bear. For years doctors had tried to convince Cedric that he wasn't the cause of his brother's condition, but facts were facts. Twenty-seven years ago, when they'd shared a womb, Cedric had stolen nearly all of the nutrients, leaving none for his brother's brain and body to properly develop. It could have just as easily been *him* in this wheelchair, living *his* life vicariously through his brother, the way Derek lived vicariously through Cedric.

Before Cedric could get a single word in, Derek started a slurred but enthusiastic recounting of every single play of yesterday's game. As he listened to his brother's excited monologue, Cedric could only marvel at the strides that had been made in Derek's condition.

When he'd first found Marshall's Place, Derek was listless, bound by the confines of his wheelchair and spending most hours of the day parked in front of the television at the group home he'd lived in back in Philadelphia. Cedric had researched better care facilities for years, and he knew it was a gift straight from God when he'd been drafted by the Sabers and could afford to send Derek to Marshall's Place.

Being able to get Derek into this facility was an opportunity for atonement, at least what little he could allow himself.

As he sat patiently listening to his brother, Cedric knew there was no other option for him. He wasn't done making up for the damage he'd caused Derek.

He had to remain a New York Saber. It was as simple as that.

## Chapter 5

$A$s she made her way through the wide concrete corridor toward the Sabers locker room, Payton mulled over the difference a couple of weeks—not to mention a legitimate reason for being there—could make. The last time she'd made this journey, her knees had felt like water and she'd been sure she would have to financially support Susan Renee after her dear friend was fired for loaning Payton her press pass.

Today, no one questioned her presence as she entered the Sabers's sacred domain. Agents were allowed to move freely in and out of the locker room. Payton nodded at David Sage, one of the few fellow agents she'd met and actually liked. He held a cell phone to his ear with his right hand, had another in his left and a third clipped to his belt. David gave her a slight wave as he passed her on his way out of the locker room.

"One day," Payton said under her breath. She'd

warrant multiple phones one of these days. For now, she was fine with her solitary BlackBerry.

She spotted Cedric as soon as he exited the shower room, his white T-shirt plastered to his muscular chest.

*Don't stare. Do* not *stare.*

"How was practice?" she greeted, triple-dog-daring her eyes to drift below his neck.

He shrugged a shoulder, which Payton knew would cause all those muscles to ripple even more. She *so* wanted to look. Pretending the sight of his outrageously sculpted body didn't affect her was getting harder by the minute.

"It was good," Cedric answered, motioning for her to follow him out of the locker room. "We had to stop early so they could repair a part of the field that got messed up during the game this weekend. I hope the city has that water main fixed by tomorrow. We need to be at our regular practice facility."

The Sabers, like every other NFL team, had a separate practice facility with a full-length football field, state-of-the-art weight rooms and everything else needed to help keep their players in tip-top shape. Payton had yet to set foot in the Sabers facility. A major break in the city's main water line had relegated them to practicing at the stadium for the past couple of weeks, which was inconvenient, since they shared the stadium with New York's other NFL team.

"So what's up with my endorsements? Am I rolling like Tiger Woods or what?" Cedric asked.

"Ha ha," Payton drawled.

"You're the one who said you were going to land an endorsement deal by the end of today."

The grin on his face was nearly as irresistible as

that muscular chest Payton was still having a hard time ignoring. She should have known he would throw the overconfident claim she'd made during their postgame brainstorming session in her face. She'd crisscrossed the city, going from storefront to storefront like a door-to-door salesman, determined to make good on her promise.

And she had.

"Have you ever eaten at Gianni's Pizza?" she asked.

"Sure." He nodded at a maintenance guy driving a golf cart piled high with shoulder pads. "Matter of fact, we had a couple of pizzas delivered last Sunday night while we played dominoes. There's one just a few blocks from Torrian's place."

So *those* were the plans he'd had last Sunday night. Payton didn't want to explore why knowing he was at Torrian's instead of on a date was such a relief, but it didn't take a genius to figure it out. Just the thought of him cavorting with one of the many women he'd been linked to over the years made her chest tighten with unease.

She needed to squelch this unhealthy fixation on his love life. As long as it did not compromise his image, Cedric was free to date any woman he wanted. Yet even as she said the words to herself, a disturbing weight settled in Payton's stomach.

"What about Gianni's?" he asked.

"You're their new spokesman. You'll be signing autographs for an hour at their original location in Brooklyn on Wednesday afternoon."

Cedric stopped and turned to face her. "Gianni's Pizza?" he said with the enthusiasm of a slug. "Are you serious?"

"I know it's not Reliant, but—"

"But nothing," he said. "Look, there's something you need to keep in mind, Payton. I'm one of the premier running backs in the National Football League. There are first-year rookies who wouldn't stoop so low as to endorse a neighborhood pizza joint."

"They are not just a pizza joint! Gianni's is a legend in this city. Every New Yorker has had a slice of their pizza at least once in their lifetime."

"How would you know? You told me you've been here less than a year."

"The owner assured me," Payton stated. "Come on, Cedric. They're going to take a couple of pictures for their advertisements and you'll sign a few autographs. This is a good start."

He still didn't look convinced, but then a corner of his mouth lifted with a reluctant smile. "To be honest, I'm kind of impressed. No agent is expected to land an endorsement deal this quickly."

Payton allowed herself to enjoy his praise for a moment before dropping the other shoe. "Okay," she continued. "So, this isn't exactly your *normal* endorsement deal."

He eyed her with a curious stare. "What isn't exactly *normal* about it?"

"Well, with most endorsement deals you get paid."

"Oh, come *on,* Payton," he groused.

She held her hands out, pleading for understanding. "Gianni's Harlem location sponsors the touch football team at the Linden Avenue rec center. The owner was there when I went to talk to the center's director about the mini-football camp and when he heard you would be there, he was beyond excited. They can't afford to hire a big-time celebrity to endorse their restaurants, and he's your biggest fan."

"Of course he is," Cedric drawled.

"Is it really such a hardship? You've been such a sport about this so far. I thought partnering with another company who helps out the rec center would add to the good press you'll get for participating in the mini-camp."

"I've been meaning to ask, is the date for the camp set in stone?"

"Yes," she said. "I talked to the center's director this morning. Permission slips went out to all the kids today. Is there something wrong with the date?"

He shrugged. "It's just that a bunch of the players usually spend the bye weekend in Atlantic City."

Payton threw her hands up in the air. "Atlantic City? Seriously? After everything we discussed about keeping you out of trouble, you make plans to spend your weekend off in Atlantic City? Do you honestly think you'll go there and stay out of trouble, Cedric?"

It was when she paused to take a breath that Payton noticed the smile edging his lips. "You're lying," she accused, ready to slap the smile from his all-too-handsome face. She pointed a finger at him. "Another rule, no rattling your agent just to get a rise out of her."

His shoulders shook with laughter. "You make it so easy. And enjoyable. It doesn't take much to imagine you battling some lawyer in court."

"I studied contract law. I was hardly ever in court," she said. She cracked a mischievous grin. "I have been told I'm pretty scary when it comes to negotiations, though."

"Perfect trait for an agent," he said.

His dark brown eyes crinkled at the corners, and her pulse quickened with a sudden burst of awareness. She wasn't sure when he'd come to stand so close. Just as she wasn't certain of when the corridor had become so quiet. The absence of noise only intensified the sound of their breathing.

"So you'll be at Gianni's on Wednesday, right?" she asked, taking a step back.

Cedric stared at her for several long moments, the gleam in his eyes telling Payton he found her retreat amusing. "If my agent says I need to be at Gianni's on Wednesday, that's where I'll be."

Payton was about to respond when movement over his shoulder caught her eye. "What's going on over there?" She moved toward a tunnel that was an offshoot to the one underneath the stadium.

Cedric turned. "Probably the guys still resodding the turf."

"I want to see it," Payton said on an awe-filled breath. Not waiting for Cedric, she drifted through the arched hallway that led to the field, stopping just at the edge of the neatly trimmed deep green grass. She debated whether she should slip off her shoes before stepping onto it.

She went for it. Leaving her shoes behind, Payton stepped onto an actual NFL football field for the very first time. She turned in a slow circle and marveled at the sheer size of the place. On any given Sunday, seventy thousand people filled these seats. That was ten times the number of people in her small hometown.

She closed her eyes and sucked in a deep breath, soaking in the moment. The freshly cut grass was cool beneath her feet. It tickled her through her sheer stockings.

She pulled in another deep breath and allowed the smell to bring her back to the sideline at Manchac High

School. If she concentrated, she could hear her father's deep voice booming from the sidelines. Coach Moe, as he was known throughout Manchac, could instill fear in his players with just a look. When he barked an order in that commanding voice, everyone jumped to attention.

Payton's fists clenched at her sides as she tried desperately to hold on to the memory. She was so afraid that one day she would wake up and not be able to recall her daddy's voice.

She wouldn't allow that to happen. She couldn't. Her memories were all she had left. And her love of football. It was a special bond they'd shared that Payton would always treasure.

Finally, *finally,* her hard work had landed her exactly where she needed to be. Close to the game they both loved.

Coach Moe would be proud.

Cedric hovered at the edge of the field, leaning against the wall of the tunnel he'd run through dozens of times over the past four years. As he watched Payton stand there in silent worship, he tried to recall a single time he'd felt the sheer joy he saw on her face. She was relishing this. He could feel it radiating from her like warmth from the sun.

Cedric knew he was lucky. Millions of young boys dreamed of playing in the NFL and only a fraction ever got the chance to experience that reality. He'd never taken this gift for granted, but not once had he approached the football field with such reverence. At that moment, he knew if Payton Mosely had been born male, she would have been playing in the NFL. That was the kind of love for the game he saw on her face.

What was it about this woman and football? Where had this passion—this obsession—come from? Cedric was torn between flooding her with the dozen questions swirling in his mind or just watching her as she enjoyed something as simple as standing on a football field.

She turned in a slow circle, her face pointed up as she took in the tens of thousands of empty seats. She stopped when she saw him and smiled.

"This is so cool," she mouthed.

Cedric pushed away from the wall and walked onto the field. He looked around the stadium, trying to see it for the first time through the eyes of someone who would never get to play the game, but who, without a doubt, loved it as much as he did.

"It is awesome, isn't it?" he agreed.

"What's it like to play here?" Her eyes were luminous with the same excitement that came through her voice. "I can only imagine how loud the crowd is to you guys on the field. To have all those fans cheering and screaming. It must be amazing!"

Cedric stuck his hands in his pockets to stop himself from touching her. He was once again struck by how beautiful she was. Even more startling was the contradiction she presented. Gorgeous, petite, feminine women usually didn't live and breathe football. Cedric honestly could not think of anything sexier.

"The best ever was my first playoff game as a Saber," he started, answering her question. "This place was electric. I'd played in bowl games in college, but I doubt if anything will ever compare to running through the tunnel before that first playoff game. I just remember the fog from the smoke machines as we ran onto the field, and then the teal and silver confetti that was everywhere after we won. I found confetti in places confetti should never be found," he joked.

Payton burst out laughing. The sound was more magical than the cheer of all Sabers fans combined.

She stared at him with rapt attention, complete and utter wonder shining in her eyes. "It sounds marvelous," she said.

"You really do love this game, don't you?"

Her eyes softened around the edges. "I do." She let out a soft laugh. "When I was a little girl, I would kneel next to my bed and say my prayers at night. And they always ended the same way. 'God, please let girls play football.'"

Cedric's chest tightened with pity for the little girl who never got her prayer answered.

"There's nothing I wanted to do more," she confessed. "One of my first memories is being on my daddy's shoulders while he yelled at his players to keep their legs up as they ran sprints. I was probably two years old. I spent nearly every afternoon on his shoulders until I was six."

"What happened when you turned six that you had to stop going to their practices?"

"Oh, no. I never stopped going. I'd just gotten too heavy to be on my dad's shoulders. I had to settle for standing next to him on the sideline. I had my own whistle and clipboard. The guys on the team even got me a Manchac Mustangs cap with 'Coach Moe, Jr.' embroidered on the side."

Cedric couldn't keep the smile from tracing across his lips. He could just imagine a six-year-old Payton barking at a bunch of hefty high school players five times her size. He'd bet they all fell in line when she talked, too.

"My dad would have loved this," she continued. "No one loved football as much as he did."

"Did he play for the Longhorns? You said you were from Texas, right?"

"Yeah, from West Texas." She studied the goalpost. "Dad never played. He was born with a heart defect. You'd never know it by looking at him. He was six foot five and two-hundred-eighty pounds of muscle. But you don't have to play the game to love it."

Cedric couldn't help it. He reached out and captured her hand, the feel of her soft skin sending a shock of desire through his bloodstream.

"No, you don't," he said. He could see that now. Payton would never play football, but she loved it as much as any of the players on the Sabers squad. Cedric had no doubt about that.

Their gazes met and his heart turned over in his chest.

She averted her eyes, glancing at their intertwined hands. Cedric's palm tingled where it touched her. He ached to bring her fingers to his lips and satisfy the yearning to taste her skin. But after another long moment she lifted her gaze and pulled away.

"So," Payton said, rubbing her arms as if she were cold. "Can you handle Gianni's on your own Wednesday or do you need me to be there?"

Awareness of her lingered on his fingertips. He knew he shouldn't have touched her, but he'd *had* to. The desire had been too hard to fight.

He was a bit taken aback by her suggestion to join him at the pizza parlor. Gus Houseman had never offered to accompany him anywhere. He was always too busy with his other clients.

"If you want to drop by Gianni's, that would be fine," Cedric answered.

"I'll try to make it. It will all depend on how my schedule looks by midweek. I have something else I'm working on that may have me tied up."

"Is this 'something else' something I should know about?"

"Not yet." She shook her head. "I don't want to get your hopes up. But I promise to call you as soon as I have something more solid to go on. Just trust me."

"You say that as if it's so simple," Cedric teased, trying to diffuse some of the awkwardness that had sprouted between them after he'd touched her. Even though he was aching to touch her again.

"Ouch!" Payton laughed. "Have a little faith in your agent, Mr. Reeves."

Her words struck a chord inside him that pushed all joking aside. Cedric looked her in the eyes, the weight of everything that was at stake suddenly smothering him.

"I'm putting all of my faith in my agent."

## Chapter 6

Payton sipped from the crystal tumbler she'd been given when she first sat in the main conference room of Morrison Products. The water had grown lukewarm, while the tempers on the other side of the table had risen even higher. The VP of marketing and the company's chief operating officer were at odds over the deal, and to Payton's surprise, the men were actually allowing her to witness it.

In practicing law, you never let the opposing counsel observe any dissention in the ranks. Morrison Products's upper management seemed to have missed the day they taught that rule in business school. The COO was ready to pull the offer off the table but the marketing VP was still fighting. Apparently, Cedric's bad-boy reputation didn't faze him. The man seemed determined to make a deal with his favorite Sabers player.

Payton kept her cool. She'd decided before ever

stepping through these doors the dollar figure she would accept in order to make Cedric the new spokesman for Soft Touch Shaving Cream. They had passed that figure twenty minutes ago.

But what kind of agent would she be if she didn't try to get as much for her client as possible? She'd given Morrison Products a number that was twenty-five percent more than the amount she was actually willing to settle for, and she would not bite until they reached it.

Matt Shuster, the marketing guy, folded his hands on the table and leveled Payton with a shrewd stare. "One million, one hundred and fifty thousand," he said.

Payton lifted her glass to her lips once more, hoping the men across the table could not see the water shaking in her unsteady hands.

This was one of those defining moments that would dictate how she was perceived as an agent. If she backed down from the amount she'd requested she'd always be seen as a pushover, an agent who could be bullied. On the other hand, if she continued to play hardball, she could potentially walk away from over a million dollars for her client.

Payton's heart pumped a thousand miles per second. Her leg had begun shaking in a nervous rhythm, but she willed it to stop. She refused to show a modicum of fear. Since the minute she'd sat at this table, she'd fallen back into lawyer mode. These two had nothing on the opposing counsels and judges she'd faced in the Texas civil court system.

"Well, gentlemen," she said, pushing her chair back from the table. "I thank you for your time today. But I'm afraid I can't accept this offer."

Matt Shuster's jaw dropped open.

"You're going to leave over fifty thousand dollars?" Louis Crane, the COO, asked, his voice incredulous.

Payton leveled her gaze on the balding man who had given her the toughest fight she'd had since her days of practicing law. "A better question is 'are you going to lose Cedric Reeves over fifty thousand dollars?'" She braced her hands on the table and started to rise.

"Fine," Louis Crane said.

Payton did her best to stop a smile from creeping onto her lips as she lowered herself back into the chair. She'd done it! She'd played hardball with these shrewd, intimidating businessmen and won. If this was the bliss she had to look forward to as a sports agent, Payton had no doubt she'd chosen the right career. The past hour had been the ultimate rush.

Payton refused to allow any emotion to show on her face until she slipped behind the wheel of her car and squealed like a child. She smiled the entire hour it took to make it back to her apartment in New Jersey. She smiled as she loaded two weeks' worth of laundry into mesh laundry bags and packed them into her backseat.

She was still smiling several hours later when her cell phone rang. She checked the caller ID and her smile widened even more at the name that appeared.

"So, how was it?" she asked, balancing her cell phone between her ear and shoulder. She stuffed the mix of jeans, T-shirts, underwear and bath towels into the washing machine, thinking of the different ways her mother would kill her if she ever found out Payton did laundry without separating it into proper batches.

"It was better than the folks at Gianni's expected," Cedric answered. "The place was packed. The restaurant manager said they did more business in that one hour than they had ever done on an entire Wednesday."

"That's awesome," Payton said. "I really wanted to be there but I was busy with that 'little something else' I mentioned on Monday. I've got some news for you," she continued, unable to keep the enthusiasm from her voice.

"Reliant?" was Cedric's excited response.

Payton rolled her eyes. He sure knew how to let the air out of her balloon. "No, not Reliant," she lamented. "Would you forget about them for a while? I told you Reliant Sportswear will take time."

"Sorry," Cedric answered, contriteness coloring his voice. "What's the news?"

"I got you another endorsement deal."

"A real one?"

"Of course a real one."

"One where I actually get paid?" he clarified.

"Yes," Payton said with a long-suffering sigh. She added quarters to the washing machine and turned it on, then returned to the folding table where the load she'd removed from the dryer sat in a heap. Maybe with the Soft Touch deal she could finally afford a place with a washer and dryer.

"So who's the deal with?" Cedric asked.

"You, Mr. Reeves, are the new face of Soft Touch Shaving Cream," she announced.

There was a pause, then, "Shaving cream?"

Incredulousness oozed from his end of the phone. Payton clutched her fist around the rayon top she was about to fold, wishing for a moment it was her client's neck.

"This is good, Cedric. It's a national campaign, and I got them to add twenty-five percent to their initial offer."

"Which comes out to?"

"One point two million," she said with way more gaiety than a professional sports agent should display. Forget being professional; she got twenty percent of that money. Payton saw her mountain of student loans crumbling right before her eyes.

Adjusting the cell phone, she folded a bath sheet and added it to the laundry basket piled with clean clothes.

"Cedric, you still there?" Payton asked after several beats of silence.

"Sorry," he answered. "I was still digesting the news."

"So, you're good with this?"

"You just got me a seven-figure endorsement deal. What do you think?"

For a minute she'd thought he would throw the deal right back in her face. Compared to his teammates who had sneaker and video game endorsements, shaving cream was small potatoes. But it was a start. It showed that someone was willing to see past Cedric's bad-boy reputation and take a chance on him. All Cedric had to do was live up to the model player she'd painted him to be in her negotiations with the people from Morrison Products.

"So, what's next?" Cedric asked.

"First, you sign the contract. Then there's a commercial shoot they'd like you to do as soon as possible."

"When do I sign?" he asked.

"I can email the contract so you can read over it."

"Have you read it?" he asked.

"Of course I have."

"Then that's good enough for me."

The blanket of trust that came through with that one statement threw Payton off kilter. She wanted his trust. It was a necessity if their working relationship was going to be a successful one. But with his trust came a rush of responsibility Payton had, up until this point, not fully comprehended.

Cedric's career was in her hands. He was entrusting her with everything he'd worked years to attain. The enormity of it settled upon her chest like a crushing boulder.

"Do you have the contract with you?" Cedric asked. "I'm in Jersey, on my way from practice. I can come over and sign it. You're in Weehawken, right?"

"Yes," Payton said, thinking how truly weird it was that she knew where Cedric worked, lived and even some of his favorite restaurants, yet he wasn't even sure what city she lived in. She really *had* been stalking him. "I'll be at the laundromat at the corner of Palisade and Thirty-Ninth for another hour," she finished.

"I can be there in twenty minutes. And, Payton?"

"Yes?"

"Good job."

"Thank you," Payton answered, pride blooming in her chest. She *had* done a good job. She had not realized Cedric's praise would mean so much, but it did. It was the first dose of validation she'd received since becoming his agent. Sure, landing Cedric as a client had been a big deal, but having a client meant nothing if you couldn't make anything happen for him.

Today, Payton had made things happen.

She smiled to herself in the middle of the crowded laundromat as she recalled the rush of adrenaline she'd experienced in the meeting room at Morrison Products. On the outside it had seemed like an unfair fight—two distinguished businessmen in two-thousand-dollar suits against one petite female—but she'd come out on top.

Her real challenge would be making sure Cedric didn't do anything to blemish the new reputation she was trying to create for him. But she'd do that, too, even if she had to stick to him like glue for the rest of the football season.

Cedric made the block three times before finding a spot that had just been vacated not too far from the laundromat. He did a bad job of parallel parking his SUV, but hey, he'd grown up in South Philly; the city bus had been his way around town.

He pocketed his keys as he rounded the corner, spotting Payton through the laundromat's smudged glass window. She was standing in front of a metal table, folding a bath towel. Cedric paused to take a much-needed breath before entering the building. His heart had predictably started racing as soon as he saw her. He'd been trying to fight this…this *thing* he had for his agent, but some things were too damn strong to fight.

This was the absolute last thing he needed to deal with right now. Payton was his agent, and to Cedric's immense satisfaction, she was turning out to be a very good one. She'd shown him in the past couple of weeks that she was the real deal. And landing him a seven-figure endorsement deal today had solidified that fact… even if the deal was for shaving cream.

It was vital that his and Payton's relationship remain professional. He could *not* mess this up.

But he couldn't deny what he was feeling, either. He was attracted to her. No, it was more than that.

He *wanted* her.

Cedric cursed under his breath. What the hell had he expected to happen? That she was hotter than Philly in July was reason enough to want to get with her. Add in the fact that Payton knew football like no one else's business, and he was toast.

*And* she had a sense of humor—a real one, not just a fake giggle like the other women he'd dated, who'd only laughed at things they thought he found funny. Payton was as real as it got. How could he not want her?

"She's your agent," he reminded himself. That should banish any amorous feelings he had toward her. "Yeah, right," Cedric muttered.

With another deep breath, he opened the door to the laundromat and slipped inside. As he'd anticipated, Cedric was instantly recognized by the dozen or so people doing their laundry. Over the past four years he'd become accustomed to signing autographs when he was out in public.

When he finally made his way to Payton, she'd moved to one of the mega-size dryers along the wall.

"Having fun with your legion of fans?" she asked with a sly grin.

"The life of a superstar," he drawled with a hint of self-mockery. "It comes with the territory."

She rolled her eyes, her grin growing broader. Cedric tried to help with the armful of laundry she retrieved from the dryer, but she said, "I've got it," and headed for the folding tables that lined the left wall.

"Tell me about today," she called over her shoulder.

"I signed autographs and ate pizza," he answered. "You tell me about this new endorsement deal."

A piece of laundry fell as she deposited the load onto the table. Payton reached for it but Cedric caught it before it reached the floor. He fingered the garment, a silky number with skinny straps and lace. His gut clinched at the thought of her wearing it.

Payton snatched the top from his hand and stuffed

it in a basket of folded laundry, but the look, the feel, even the smell of it were already branded in his brain. Imagining the silken fabric flowing over her skin brought on a blitz of erotic images. All he could think about was peeling the piece of lingerie from her body.

A red hue bloomed on her cheeks. She cleared her throat several times, folding a utilitarian white T-shirt that turned him on for the simple fact that it had at some point touched her skin.

"So," she said with a slight shake in both her voice and her fingers that fumbled with the T-shirt.

She was flustered. And it was sexy as hell. Cedric couldn't help but think of other ways he could make her body blush.

"The endorsement deal," Payton said, glancing at him then quickly averting her eyes.

"Yes," he replied, even though he was having a hell of a time concentrating on business with all of her sexy unmentionables within arm's reach. "How did this endorsement deal come about?"

"I got a tip from an old college friend who heard that Soft Touch was thinking of going the celebrity endorsement route," Payton explained. "He set up a meeting with their marketing department. We've been going back and forth for the past couple of weeks."

"The past couple of weeks? We've only been working together for a couple of weeks," he said.

"I was being proactive," Payton said, folding a washcloth into a neat square.

"And pretty confident." Cedric chuckled. "What would you have done if I had refused to work with you?"

"I never let myself think it," Payton admitted. "I was

determined to wear you down. And aren't you happy I did?"

Her smile was infectious. It did things to Cedric that caused the blood to stir hot in his veins. Then she pulled another silky piece of lingerie from the pile of clothing, this one black satin. Cedric's blood went from a simmer to boiling over.

"Very happy," he answered, staring at her lips.

Her smile faltered. "Don't," Payton whispered, but she didn't back away. Her breaths were short, her chest rising and falling. Cedric moved closer.

Now she backed away.

"Stop it, Cedric." She put a hand up. "I told you when we first agreed to work together that it would be strictly business. We can't do this."

"But you want to." Cedric dared her to deny it.

Her smoky eyes lowered to the table before rising back to meet his gaze. "We *can't*," she emphasized. She reached into the briefcase next to the laundry basket and retrieved a sheaf of folded papers. "Now, please, just sign the contract." She turned to a page flagged with a yellow sticky note.

Not even bothering to read it, Cedric snatched the pen she held out to him and scrawled his name across the contract. She'd earned his trust. Cedric had no doubts that she had his best interests at heart.

Besides, they had something just as important to talk about.

"Why can't there be more between us?" he asked her. Cedric knew he should back off but something inside him refused to accept her answer. "It's not as if there's an official rule against it."

"I don't care about official rules. Getting romantically

involved with you would undermine me as an agent. Did you ever try hitting on Gus Houseman?"

Cedric was onto her little diversion tactic. She brought up Gus whenever she was trying to distract him from herself, but Cedric wasn't letting her get away with it this time. She wasn't Gus Houseman in any way, shape or form. She worked harder than Gus did. She treated him with more respect than Gus ever had. And she sure as hell was sexier than Gus could ever hope to be.

"If Gus looked anything like you do, I would have tried," he answered.

"This isn't going to happen," she said.

"Convince me," he dared her, stepping closer, pinning her between himself and the metal table. The contact lit his body on fire.

Payton's breaths came in rapid, sexy pants.

She pulled in a shallow breath and said, "Cedric, please don't ruin this for me."

It was the pleading in her voice that made him back away.

Her chest heaved with a shaky sigh, her hand still clenching the silky lingerie that Cedric knew he would dream about for at least a week. She finally raised her eyes to meet his and what he saw there made him want to throw her denial right back in her face.

Regret. Longing. Desire.

She wanted him just as much as he wanted her.

But Payton was right, he reluctantly admitted to himself. They couldn't compromise their relationship as agent and client. It was an invitation for trouble.

"I'm sorry," Cedric said, knowing an apology was necessary but not feeling the words. The only thing he was sorry for was the fact that they couldn't explore this desire that was shooting between them like sparks from a bonfire.

"But you know it's here. You feel it. This…this attraction between us." Even as he said the word, Cedric knew it was inadequate. Attraction didn't begin to describe what he was feeling. It didn't fully capture what he saw in Payton's eyes. This was so much more than a simple attraction.

He took a cautious step toward her, not trusting himself to keep his hands off of her. Mindful of the other people in the laundromat, Cedric kept his voice low. "I know you said we have to be strictly about business, and I understand why. Remember, I've got just as much at stake here as you do. But how can you deny what's going on between us, Payton?" he asked. "How long do you plan to fight it?"

She closed her eyes, her chest rising and falling with a profound breath. When she opened her eyes, the desire Cedric had seen there had been replaced by something else. Resolve.

"I'm going to fight it for as long as I have to," she answered. "And so will you. It's not an option, Cedric. It's the way it has to be."

She shouldered past him, leaving him with a mountain of disappointment.

# Chapter 7

Payton's eyes darted from the email on her BlackBerry to the foot traffic in front of her as she made her way up Eighth Avenue. The past week and a half had been ridiculously busy, but at least she was running only an hour behind schedule today.

She stopped at a hot dog vendor, promising herself this was her last hot dog of the week. She would make time for lunch tomorrow if it killed her. That is, if the hot dogs didn't do it first.

Her cell phone trilled just as she walked up to the nondescript building at Eighth and Thirty-Fifth. Payton stopped short at the sight of the familiar number that illuminated the tiny screen. It was the main switchboard number for McNamara and Associates, the firm where she'd practiced law back in Austin. Payton stared at the phone a few moments before it even occurred to her she should answer it. Why were they calling her? She hadn't talked to anyone from her old firm in nearly a year.

"Mosely," she answered.

"Payton! How are things going?" came Daniel McNamara's booming voice.

"Daniel, how are you?"

"Good. Everything's good here. Better than good, actually," he said. "We've got some exciting things happening at the firm."

"That's wonderful to hear," Payton said, looking up and down Eighth Avenue. She needed to get inside. The taping of Cedric's shaving cream commercial had begun nearly an hour ago. "Well, thanks for calling," she said, trying to end the conversation.

"How would you like to become a partner?" Daniel asked abruptly, and Payton nearly swallowed her tongue.

"A partner? Daniel…I…I'm no longer practicing law," she said.

"Come on, Payton." Her ex-boss chuckled. The condescension in his voice had the effect of fingernails scraping down a chalkboard. "You've had some time to do your sports agent thing, but you're a lawyer, one of the best this firm has. We need you to head up negotiations. It's time you got back to doing real work."

"Had," Payton clarified. "You no longer have me, and I am doing real work," she annunciated through clenched teeth. "In fact, I'm late for a meeting with my client. He's currently shooting a commercial for the sponsor with whom I've orchestrated a seven-figure deal for him. So, yes, Daniel, I *am* working. Thanks for the call." She mashed down the End button.

Payton paced outside the building, swearing under her breath. She would not allow Daniel's out-of-the-blue phone call to trip her up today. She was here to give her client support; her sole focus right now should be on Cedric.

She set the ring tone on her phone to silent, slipped it into her purse and entered the building. She checked in at the security desk and was buzzed in and directed to the bank of elevators.

She returned the nod of the guy who stepped onto the elevator behind her, then stared at the illuminated numbers above the door. Unable to stop herself, Payton grabbed her phone from her purse and checked it once more just to make sure Daniel hadn't tried to call her again.

She wasn't just checking to see if he'd called, Payton realized. She was *hoping* he had.

Daniel's offer had been a curveball she had not been expecting. McNamara and Associates was one of the largest firms in central Texas, with over a thousand associates. The negotiations section housed nearly a hundred of those lawyers. And he wanted her to head that division?

Was there any division head under the age of thirty-five? Would she be the first one? She was heady with thoughts of the prestige the appointment would bring. Not only that, if she went back to practicing law, there would be nothing standing in the way of exploring the white-hot attraction between her and Cedric.

Payton banished both thoughts from her mind.

*You are a sports agent,* she reminded herself. She had a client now, one for whom she'd just garnered a respectable endorsement deal. This was what she wanted, what she'd been working for. What was she thinking to give Daniel McNamara even a single moment's consideration?

The elevator door opened on the twenty-eighth floor, and Payton put thoughts of McNamara and Associates out of her mind. She walked up to the receptionist.

"I'm Payton Mosely. I'm here for the Soft Touch commercial shoot."

The receptionist handed her a sign-in sheet. "It's in suite three." She pointed down a hallway.

"Do I just walk in?" Payton asked.

The girl clicked her computer mouse and said, "Doesn't look like they've started yet. The shoot before this one ran a little behind. Go right ahead. As long as the light above the door is green it's safe for you to walk in."

When she reached the door to suite three, Payton edged it open and stepped into another world on the other side. There were at least a dozen people running about the large, mostly bare room. Three large cameras made a triangle around a bathroom mock-up. Large spotlights shone down on a white pedestal sink and an oval mirror hanging on a freestanding wall.

"Are you Payton?" Payton turned to find a young woman wearing a headset and sticking her hand out. "Hi, I'm Tammy. I'm the production assistant on today's shoot. I was told to look out for you."

"Sorry I'm so late," Payton apologized.

"That's okay. You're actually right on time. Cedric is just getting out of makeup. We should start shooting within the next few minutes. I'll show you where you can watch."

Cedric stepped out from behind a faux wall and Payton's mouth went dry.

"Oh, Lord," she whispered under her breath. He was bare-chested, his skin glistening under the intense lights.

He had a plush light blue towel riding low on his hips. Standing there in his bare feet, looking as if he'd just walked out of the shower, it was all too easy for Payton to picture him looking this way under entirely different circumstances. Much more enjoyable circumstances.

"You made it," Cedric called as he started toward her.

"Just in time," Payton said, her heart pumping faster as he approached. "Sorry I'm late. I've been swamped today."

"Hey, when you're making me money, you can take as long as you want." He turned and called to another woman wearing a headset. "Georgia, this is my agent, Payton Mosely. Georgia is the director," Cedric explained.

Georgia shook her hand, then bellowed, "Okay, people, let's get in position. Even though they were a half hour late in turning over the studio, they still want us out on time. You know what that means, right?" She directed her question at Cedric.

"That I don't have many chances for mistakes," he answered. "I guess it's a good thing I only have two lines." Cedric turned back to her. "This won't take long," he said, giving Payton a wink that set her stomach aflutter.

"Where's Alana?" Georgia called.

"I'm here," came a voice from behind the partition. Seconds later, a model-thin woman with mile-long legs, gorgeous, chestnut hair and a face worthy of a thousand magazine covers, appeared, wearing a silk robe that stopped midthigh and belted loosely at her waist.

Payton's stomach tanked. No one had mentioned a

female counterpart when she'd discussed the specifics of the commercial shoot. A disturbing quake of uneasiness swept through her as she watched the woman sidle up to Cedric and intertwine her arm with his.

"Sorry," the actress said in a voice that sounded like someone who'd just finished the New York Marathon in record time. "We can get started."

Georgia's call for action was the start of the most tortuous forty-five minutes Payton had experienced in a long time.

Even though Cedric delivered his two lines flawlessly, Georgia continued to find fault in the lighting, in Cedric's stance, in the tiny streaks of shaving cream left on his face when the actress swiped at his jaw with the razor.

And through every take, Payton had to suffer through Alana running her red-tipped nails along Cedric's washboard abs and whispering playfully in his ear. Every grin he turned on the gorgeous actress caused a painful ache to twist through Payton's gut.

She found her eyes zeroing in on Cedric's chest in all its naked glory. His body was magnificently sculpted. It was a by-product of the job, she supposed, but Payton had seen enough ballplayers on television to know that not all of them put as much work into their physiques. Those chiseled pectorals and biceps that looked like smooth boulders came from more than just your normal workout. Cedric put in the extra effort, and Soft Touch Shaving Cream's target audience—along with the world's entire female population—were among the lucky benefactors of all that hard work.

Not to mention Alana, who seemed to be striving for an Oscar in the Best Flirting by a Half-Naked

Woman category. Payton had to fight the urge to break
the actress's finger when she swiped a bit of lingering
white foam from Cedric's cheek. They both laughed
at something he had said, and the sinking feeling in
Payton's stomach reached a new, painful level.

*This is Cedric Reeves,* she reminded herself.

Over the course of the past couple of weeks, her mind
had managed to rub a shiny coat over Cedric's tarnished
playboy reputation, but as she watched him openly flirt
with Alana, thoughts of other women he'd been linked
to in the past bombarded her. How could she possibly
think there could ever be anything between herself and
Cedric, especially when he had his pick of some of the
most beautiful women in the world at his fingertips?

Payton quickly reined in the feelings of insecurity
that had begun to surface. She may not be *Vogue*
cover material, but she wasn't in the running for *MAD*
magazine, either. The fact that Cedric was used to
fashion model types worked in her favor. She could stop
obsessing over this ridiculous attraction to him, and get
back to focusing on Mosely Sports Management.

Despite her mental pep talk, Payton couldn't deny
the ache in her chest as she witnessed the easy rapport
between Cedric and Alana. Falling for him would be
akin to diving headfirst into a pool of heartache.

When the director called cut for the seventh time,
numerous groans floated around the studio, with
Cedric's being one of the loudest. He looked over at
Payton and made a choking gesture with his hands, but
then he smiled at her and Payton's chest grew tight.

It was just a smile, she told herself. She would ignore
it the same way she tried to ignore everything else
about the way he affected her. But it was becoming

more difficult by the day. Ever since that incident in the laundromat when she'd been so close to giving in to her desire, Payton had had a hard time picturing Cedric as just a client.

He was a man. And it had been a long time since she'd allowed herself to feel anything for one of those.

The director started take number eight, and Payton could practically hear the prayers in everyone's mind that this one would be *the* one. Cedric once again delivered his lines flawlessly and Alana played the part of sexy girlfriend to perfection. Less than two minutes after it had begun, the take was over.

"That's a wrap," Georgia called out. Applause resounded around the studio.

Payton was hoping to make a quick escape, but as soon as the production assistant finished wiping the excess shaving cream from his face, Cedric started toward her. She braced herself for the onslaught of desire she knew would hit with his close proximity.

"So, you think I'm ready for the big screen, or what?" Cedric asked, his smile stretching from one ear to the other.

"Not sure how Hollywood will keep you out," Payton remarked with sufficient sarcasm.

"Spoken like a true agent. Tell your client any lie he needs to hear to make him happy."

"Weren't you the one who said I needed to stroke your ego? Just granting my client's wish."

He leaned in a few inches and in a low, husky voice, said, "Not all of them."

A pool of need stirred deep within Payton's belly. Her usual knack for witty comebacks deserted her, leaving her with nothing to shield the desire she knew was evident in her own eyes. All the reasons she should guard her heart against feelings for Cedric were shoved aside, making room for one undeniable fact: she wanted him.

He took a step closer, standing so near she could feel the heat radiating from his naked skin.

"You can tell me 'no' all you want, Payton. But I don't believe you mean it for a second. Let this be fair warning, I plan to wear you down until you say yes."

With that he backed away, leaving her breathless, her thoughts racing a million miles per second. His warning rang in her ears, conjuring all manner of erotic images. She could imagine the methods Cedric might use to wear her down.

And, God help her, she wanted him to use every single one.

Why was this attraction so hard to fight? With everything that was at stake, controlling any wayward feelings toward her client should have been the least of her worries. Yet thoughts of Cedric occupied most of her time. She could only presume that after today, visions of his glistening chest would stake their claim right in the middle of her dreams as well.

"Ms. Mosely." It was Tammy, the production assistant. "They're telling us we need to clear out. If you want to wait for Mr. Reeves there are several seating areas on the third floor's lobby. I can have him meet you there."

"That sounds perfect," Payton answered. "Thanks for your help today."

"Are you kidding? I got to work with a practically naked Cedric Reeves. Don't tell Georgia I said so, but I would have worked this shoot for free."

Payton laughed. She knew exactly how Tammy felt.

She had a quarter of a million dollars' payday coming

her way from Morrison Products. It seemed almost criminal to collect on something she'd taken such pleasure in.

The image of Alana running her hands up and down Cedric's chest quickly doused all those pleasurable thoughts.

She left the studio and headed for the third floor. As she lowered herself into a plush chair tucked into a corner of the well-appointed third-floor lobby area, Payton couldn't help but wish Daniel McNamara would call her back with his offer to make her a partner. Practicing law didn't seem like such a bad idea at the moment. At the very least it would help solve the quandary she faced regarding her feelings toward Cedric.

And it could very well save her from a broken heart.

Payton kept her eyes on the elevators as she answered emails and looked over appointments in her BlackBerry. She had been waiting just under twenty minutes when Cedric stepped out of one of the elevators. He was instantly approached by two men in business suits who shook his hand and patted him on the back.

Payton walked toward him but kept her distance, giving him space to spend time with his fans. As he signed an autograph, he caught her eyes across the lobby and the edge of his lips tipped up in a smile. It sent a shiver down Payton's spine. Her fingers clutched the handle of the black bag she held in front of her. She had to release some of this pent-up energy soon or she would burst.

After a full five minutes of signing autographs and talking football, Cedric made his way to where she was standing,

"Thanks for waiting," he greeted.

"We have a meeting," she answered. "We still need to go over the agenda for Saturday's mini-camp."

"Is that the only reason you waited?" he asked, his voice decidedly lower, more seductive.

Payton looked away, then looked back at him. "Cedric, why are you doing this? Why are you deliberately trying to mess up something that is working so well for both of us?" Especially when he'd just spent the better part of an hour flirting with the actress during the commercial shoot.

"Is that what you think I'm doing? Trying to mess things up? I guess I'm not as good at this as I thought I was."

"You know what I mean," Payton said.

"I hear the words, but I don't think they're what you mean, Payton. You wouldn't look at me the way you do if this was really all about business for you."

"Okay. Fine." She held up a hand up. "I find you attractive. There. I'll admit that much. I'll even go so far as to say that if things were different, if you were *not* my client, I'd be tempted to…" She tried to find the right word.

"Throw me on the floor and ravish me?" Cedric asked.

She shot him a dirty look. "I was going to say *explore* this…whatever it is that's going on here."

"So you do acknowledge that there is definitely something between us."

"Neither of us is blind, Cedric."

He took a step closer, his voice, when he spoke, bordered on pleading. "So why are you denying us when we both want it? Stop fighting this, Payton."

She crossed her arms over her chest, needing to create some kind of physical barrier between them.

"Listen up because I'm not going to explain this to you again," she said. "As long as you are my client, nothing can happen between us. And don't try firing me. You signed a contract. I'm your agent until the end of the free-agency period. So, until then…"

Payton couldn't make herself finish the sentence, which was more telling than anything she'd said so far. Just the thought of being near Cedric week after week and having to deny herself was sheer agony.

But she would do it. She *must* do it.

If she wanted to be taken seriously in this male-dominated industry, she couldn't let a girly thing like feelings get in the way. She'd already proven she could land a client and score a major endorsement deal. It was more than ninety percent of the men who'd taken the NFL Players Association's Certification Exam with her could boast. But if she were standing in a room full of men and someone was asked to point out the sports agents, Payton knew she'd be the last one picked.

She'd worked too hard and had sacrificed too much to get to this point in her career. She would not allow something as frivolous as lust to derail her well-laid plans. It was not going to get in the way.

No matter how much it killed her.

Cedric studied his agent across the table as he idly stabbed his fork into the potato salad that had come with his roast beef sandwich. She was all business right now, but Cedric had caught the look in her eyes as she'd stood against the wall observing the commercial shoot. The actress he'd been paired with had thought he was flirting with her, but every flex of his muscles had been with a single purpose in mind—to drive Payton out of her mind with wanting. Maybe then she could feel a small bit of the anguish he'd been mired in for the past few weeks.

He couldn't go on this way much longer. Despite the praise he'd received from the director today, Cedric wasn't much of an actor, and pretending that being around Payton wasn't driving him crazy with need required Academy Award-winning acting ability.

"Did any of the other players confirm they would be there to help with the camp?" she asked him as she scribbled notes onto a notepad.

"I forced a couple of the rookies to take part," he answered, dropping the fork and pushing his half-eaten sandwich aside.

"Intimidating rookies was not what I had in mind when I asked you to recruit volunteers," Payton said.

"They expect the rest of the team to push them around. It's a rite of passage," he said. "Jared said he'd help out, too. And Torrian will try to make it."

"Awesome," she said. Her eyes softened with her smile and it took everything Cedric had within him to stay on his side of the table.

Payton was the first to break eye contact. Cedric couldn't have looked away from those deep brown eyes even at the threat of gunpoint. She took a sip from her diet soda and returned her attention to the array of papers occupying the small deli table they'd commandeered nearly an hour ago.

"Let's go over the itinerary once more," she continued, all business once again. "You're going to spend the first half hour explaining a bit about the rules and history of the game, then the kids will break up into groups to run practice drills."

Cedric nodded in response.

"Then it's lunch, provided by none other than your favorite pizzeria."

"Oh, goody. I've been dying for more pizza from Gianni's," he deadpanned, earning a laugh from her. Cedric savored the sound. It was the first uninhibited response from her since their little confrontation after the commercial shoot. By some unspoken agreement their earlier skirmish had been tabled, but the basis of it continued to peck away at Cedric's brain.

They were two consenting adults. Why should it matter that she was his agent? Why should it matter what anyone else thought?

But he knew the way the world worked, and he knew exactly what people would think if he and Payton became romantically involved. Payton was right; she would lose all credibility as an agent. An even more disturbing thought was the potential for other ballplayers to think if they signed with Mosely Sports Management they would get a little something extra as part of the deal.

Cedric's hands balled into fists. He was ready to commit bodily harm just at the thought of another player thinking about Payton in that way. But he knew how those guys' minds worked. Hell, he *was* one of those guys. That was the first thing he'd thought when she'd approached him. He could not expect her to jeopardize her reputation.

But what if they were extra discreet…?

"Cedric?"

"What?" He had no idea what she'd said.

"I asked if it's okay for both girls and boys to participate in the same touch football game, or should we separate them by gender?"

"It'll be flag football," he answered. "No tackling."

"Great." She nodded. "The director said nearly all of the kids have returned their permission slips, so it looks like we'll have about thirty participants on Saturday."

"And you're going to be there?" he asked.

"In the afternoon. I'm having one of my signature coffeehouse meetings Saturday morning." She paused, a small grin creating a dimple Cedric had never noticed before. "It's with Electronic Sports Gaming," she said, her eyes lighting up.

"What?" Cedric nearly bolted out of his chair. ES Gaming was one of the hottest video game companies around. "Are you serious?"

"Don't get too excited. We're not talking the cover of *NFL Hardball* but I am hoping to get you a spot as one of the video game's premier running backs. If we're lucky, you may get to do your own voice-over in the game."

"Why didn't you tell me about this earlier?"

"Because I've just set up the meeting with them. As I said, don't get too excited yet. This is still very early."

Cedric leaned back in his chair and shook his head at the hand fate had dealt him. He'd been given exactly what he'd asked for in an agent, and now half the time he wished he could fire her so he could have her for himself.

"I've been sitting here trying to convince myself that you're not all that good of an agent just so I could justify dropping you. But you're a damn good agent."

"Thank you," she said, though her forlorn expression told him she wished things could be different as well.

This was torture. Pure and simple.

They shouldn't have to choose between one or the other. They shouldn't have to worry about what other people would say, dammit. But they did. And at this point in his career Cedric knew he needed Payton, the agent, even more than he needed Payton, the potential bed partner.

"So," he said. "You're speaking to ES Gaming on Saturday. What else do you have lined up?"

She ticked off several clothing lines, a sports drink and a car dealership, all of which she'd learned about from her web of online connections. It struck Cedric once again how different Payton was from Gus Houseman. Gus hadn't been willing to even talk endorsements, claiming it was never the right time. Cedric now realized it had never been the right time for *Gus*. He'd always been low on Gus's totem pole, coming second to his former agent's list of clients who all pulled high eight-figure salaries. Gus hadn't been concerned with furthering Cedric's career.

He needed someone out there fighting for him, getting his name in front of the people who mattered. He needed an agent who believed in him.

He needed Payton.

"Thank you," Cedric told her, because he needed to.

"For what?" she asked.

"For taking this seriously. For taking *me* seriously. I was sinking when you found me, you know? I'd called just about every major agent in the business and no one wanted to take a chance on me."

"When did it change from you taking a chance on me to the other way around?" she asked.

"When I discovered just how much I needed someone like you in my corner. As much as I want there to be something more between us—and, believe me, I want that *really* bad—I need you as my agent even more. I need you to fight for me."

Not just for him, but for his brother, Derek, too. Payton would be his key to making sure Derek could remain at Marshall's Place.

Payton reached across the table and covered his hand. She gave it a firm squeeze.

"Fight for you is exactly what I'm going to do."

# Chapter 8

Payton held a folded edition of *The Post* over her head in an attempt to shield herself from the rain that had been falling in a steady downpour for most of the day. She made sure her car doors were locked and headed for the Linden Avenue Recreation Center. Even though the mini-football camp was scheduled to end in less than an hour, Payton was relieved she was able to get here at all. Her meeting with the representative from Electronic Sports Gaming had lasted longer than she'd anticipated.

The raucous yells indicative of middle schoolers riding high on sugar and unexpended energy greeted her as she entered the rec center's front door. She wasn't sure how much Cedric and his teammates had been able to accomplish in the rain, but from the sound of things, the kids were having a great time.

Payton walked through the short entryway and into

a bevy of activity. She recognized the Sabers players instantly. Besides the fact that they were twice as tall as the room's other occupants, she'd also studied the backgrounds of each one of them. She knew the rookie linebacker, Percy Johnson, could have scored a much better deal than what his agent had gotten for him. Payton was biding her time before she approached the young player.

She spotted Cedric at what appeared to be the same time he noticed her. He jogged toward her, a half-dozen kids following in his wake.

"You made it," he greeted her.

"Barely," she replied. "It's pouring out there. But I'm here and ready for some football."

Cedric caught his lower lip between his teeth—and wasn't *that* the sexiest thing she'd seen all day. He shook his head. "Sorry, but you're too late. The flag football game ended about an hour ago."

"And we won," one of the kids who reached just past Cedric's waist said. He high-fived another little boy, while the other kids in the group glared at them. Payton figured they had been on the losing team.

"So what's left?" she asked.

"We're just running through a few more drills. These guys—"

"And girls," one of the girls said.

"Sorry." Cedric smiled down at her. "These guys and *girls* didn't know there would be a quiz at the end of today's camp," he finished.

"Quiz?"

"A test?"

The kids scurried away like bits of paper flying in the wind.

"You sure do know how to clear a room." Payton laughed.

"I was kidding about the quiz. I knew that would send them running." He grinned, looking over at the kids who had already joined the other groups. "They're a good bunch. Other than a couple of near fights over the ball, we haven't had any problems. To be honest, this is the most fun I've had in a long time."

"Better than spending your weekend off in Atlantic City?" Payton asked.

"Much better." His brown eyes sparkled with amusement. Payton was no match for their magnetic pull. He caught her gaze and held it captive. Delicious little butterflies fluttered around her stomach, and her skin tingled with sparks of the electricity that snapped between them.

"Hey, C-Man!" A little boy with crooked glasses ran up to Cedric and tugged on the hem of his shirt. "Do we really have to run sprints if we miss three passes in a row?"

Cedric's gaze finally broke away from hers. He looked over to one of the rookie wide receivers and made a cut motion, waving his hand in front of his neck.

"What? You said to make it like our normal practice," the wide receiver called.

"They're not getting paid to catch passes," Cedric replied. He returned his attention to Payton. "The rookies have been harder to handle than the kids."

"C-Man?" she asked, referring to the name the little boy had called him.

His face broke out in a grin. "Some of the kids thought I needed a nickname."

"Ah." Payton nodded. "And C-Man was the best you could come up with."

"Not me, them. We're going to call the area they sit in at the Sabers game 'C-Man's House.'"

"They're going to a Sabers game? When did this come about?"

"Not one of these kids has ever been to a game. Can you believe that? I figured what's a few tickets, you know?"

It would not be just a *few* tickets. If Payton's estimation was correct, it would probably be close to forty since he would have to provide for chaperones, or as many as sixty if each child brought a parent. Payton knew he could afford it—Cedric was a millionaire, after all—but not every player was thoughtful enough to do something like this. And she hadn't even had to tell him to do it. In fact, the idea had never crossed her mind.

"That is so generous of you," she said with a sincere smile.

Again, he shrugged it off as if it were no big deal. But it was a huge deal. The image of the partying, hotheaded, troublemaking Cedric Reeves she'd mistaken him for had been replaced by this laid-back, kindhearted person who spent an entire Saturday teaching disadvantaged kids the game of football, then promised them all tickets to a game.

Why hadn't *this* Cedric been talked about in the newspapers? Payton doubted he'd made such drastic changes just in the few weeks they'd worked together. Why had his good heart been hidden from the rest of the world?

"Are you going to make me beg?" Cedric asked.

Her brows shot up at his question.

"Your meeting? ES Gaming?" he hinted. "You've been here for ten minutes and haven't mentioned it."

"I'm sorry." Payton laughed. She should have known

he'd be itching for news. Too bad she didn't have much to share. She shrugged. "It's still too soon for me to know what will come of it. It was a good meeting. I told my contact that I was confident you would remain a New York Saber. We'll see how it goes. But these things take time."

She started toward the group of kids. "So, how can I help?"

Cedric fell into step beside her. "Help? In those clothes?"

She looked down at her gray pencil skirt that ended just above the knee and the matching cinched-waist jacket. Her black three-inch heels clickety-clacked on the rec center's painted cement floor.

"Yeah, okay. I'm not dressed for football," Payton conceded. "The bag with my sweats and sneakers is sitting next to my front door, along with my forgotten umbrella."

"Don't sweat it. We're almost done here anyway," Cedric returned. "We're going to go over a few more safety fundamentals and wrap it up."

Payton stood to the side as Cedric and his teammates huddled the kids together. In a booming voice that carried throughout the open space, Cedric imparted the importance of being safe, even when playing touch football. He then led the kids in a huddle yell, much like the ones Payton had watched the Sabers do right before the start of a game. The huddle broke apart with many high fives and laughter.

"Ms. Mosely?"

Payton turned, finding Mrs. Shipley, the rec center's director, waving her over to a side door. She pointed to a cardboard box at her feet. "This just arrived addressed to you."

"The shirts!" Payton said, running over to the box.

She had thought to order the T-shirts two days ago. She'd found a local screen printing shop and had paid for rush delivery, but the owner had emailed to say there was a possibility the shirts still would not be delivered by today. Payton ripped the packing tape from the box and fished out a teal-and-silver T-shirt.

"Those are great," Mrs. Shipley cooed.

"They did turn out pretty good," Payton agreed. "Let's go pass them out."

The kids went wild as Payton and the director began passing out their surprise T-shirts.

"Where did these come from?" Cedric asked, lifting a shirt from Payton's arm and holding it out. He read the caption. "The First Annual Cedric Reeves Mini-Football Camp?"

"I thought the kids would like a keepsake from their day," Payton explained, grinning at the group of kids, many of whom pulled their T-shirts right over the tops they were wearing.

"You thought of everything, didn't you?"

"The kids seem to like it," she said. She glanced at him, a smile tipping up her lips. "You know what this means, right?"

"What?"

"You now have to hold a *second* annual Cedric Reeves mini-camp."

He puffed out an exaggerated breath and rolled his eyes.

"Stop it." Payton gave him a playful punch on the arm. "You know you enjoyed this just as much as these kids did."

"Yeah, I did," he admitted, an adorably sheepish grin on his lips.

Mrs. Shipley announced that the bus had arrived to take the kids home. Payton had agreed to pay the rec center's bus driver extra for working on a Saturday, but with the rain pounding the sidewalks outside, she would make sure the man received a bonus. If not for him, the kids would have to walk home in this terrible weather.

The kids all said goodbye, many of them running up to Cedric to give him a hug. Payton's heart filled as she watched him give each child his undivided attention as they said goodbye.

Mrs. Shipley and another of the staff members with an umbrella guided the kids in small groups to the bus. When one of the girls dropped her knapsack, Cedric darted out into the rain for it. He grabbed it from the slick sidewalk and carried it to the bus, then rushed back into the center.

"You got any T-shirts I can fit into inside that box?" he asked her, holding out his arms. He was soaked to the bone after less than a minute in the unforgiving rain.

"Sorry," Payton said. "Unless you want to try stuffing yourself into a child's large." She held out one of the leftover T-shirts to him.

His brow lifted skeptically. "I couldn't get this over my arm."

Payton had to agree. The roped muscles of his rock-hard biceps would probably tear the T-shirt in two. But, God, he had to find something else to put on. The white Sabers shirt he wore was now plastered to his chest, outlining the smooth, solid muscles underneath.

"Hey, Cedric, we're out of here," Percy Johnson called as he and Vance Boyd, the rookie wide receiver, walked toward the side exit door, along with the rec center's other two staff members who had volunteered to help with the event.

"Thanks for coming, guys," Cedric called out to them.

"Like we had a choice," Vance returned.

Turning to her with a roguish grin, he said, "I get way too much pleasure out of giving those rookies a hard time."

A little boy with dreadlocks down his back came running from the rear of the center. "Where did everybody go?"

"Hey, little man, where have you been?" Cedric asked.

"I had to go to the bathroom."

Cedric caught him by the shoulder and shuffled him toward the door, but they were too late. The bus had already taken off.

Mrs. Shipley came through the door shaking the water off her umbrella. She stopped when she spotted the boy. "Daniel Johnson, what are you doing here?"

"Bathroom," Cedric explained. "I can take him home," he offered.

"No, I'll do it," Mrs. Shipley said. "I know where he lives. This isn't the first time he's been left behind." She motioned for the boy to follow her, but before walking back through the door, she turned to Payton and Cedric. "Ms. Mosely, I know we have a few things to discuss. Do you mind hanging around for just a bit? I won't be long."

"Sure," Payton said. "We'll start picking up some of this equipment."

Mrs. Shipley nodded and led the little boy out of the center.

Payton turned to find Cedric standing with his

arms crossed over his damp shirt. "I didn't mean to automatically include you in cleanup duty," she said. "You've been here all day. I don't expect you to stay."

"I can't think of another place I'd rather be right now," he answered in a silky voice.

Payton stopped short. She attempted to speak but for the life of her couldn't form a single response.

Cedric took a step toward her and her synapses began firing again. Payton sidestepped him and headed toward the middle of the room, where remnants of the day's activities lay strewn about. She grabbed a mesh bag that was draped across the back of a chair and began stuffing it with the pieces of uniform equipment Cedric had brought for show-and-tell.

"Looks like the kids enjoyed themselves," she said, shoving the knee pads and helmet into the bag.

"We've already had this conversation," Cedric said, his voice both amused and sexy.

The blood rushing through her veins picked up its pace. Payton tried to stuff the bulky pair of shoulder pads into the bag, but the protruding edges kept getting caught up in the bag's webbing.

"What's wrong with this thing?" she groused.

Cedric grabbed her wrists, halting her assault on the equipment. "Would you relax?" he said. "Give me this before management fines me for destroying team property."

"I'm sorry," Payton said. "It's just…" But she couldn't finish the statement. How did she verbalize what had her wound so tight? She couldn't allow Cedric to know that just being around him sapped every bit of her will to resist him. It would only encourage him to try harder, and Payton knew she was living on borrowed time when it came to fighting this attraction. If he pushed any harder, she was going to cave.

She let him handle the shoulder pads while she started picking up footballs.

"Didn't you have a couple of other guys who were supposed to help out?" Payton asked.

"Jared was here earlier, but his girlfriend called and he went running like the whipped little girl that he is."

She smiled at the thought of the big football player dropping everything to rush to his girlfriend's side. "I think that's so sweet," she said.

Cedric's right brow arched, and in a husky whisper he said, "That's good to know."

His seductively murmured words traveled along her skin like a sensual caress. Payton felt a hot flush creep up her neck. Her eyes were drawn to his mouth and that sexy dip right in the middle. As if he knew what it would do to her, his tongue darted out and wet his lips.

Payton sucked in a swift breath. The urge to kiss him was so overwhelming she had to stop herself from closing the distance between them and connecting those lips to her own.

"So, everything went okay?" she asked, for what, the third time?

"You really need to stop fighting this," Cedric said.

Payton pretended she didn't hear him. She *had* to fight this, even though it was getting harder by the millisecond to deny the intense attraction that suffused the air whenever she was around him.

She picked up another football and tossed it into the air. "I'm sorry I missed the game," she said. "I was in the mood for a little football."

Cedric cinched the drawstring on the mesh equipment

bag and shoved it to the side. He motioned for her to throw the ball. "Let me see what you've got," he said.

"You want to play football?" she asked.

He hitched a shoulder in a casual shrug. "It's what I do." He clapped his hands together, then held them out. "Come on, Ms. Football Guru. You may know a lot about the game, but there's a big difference between knowing a few plays on paper and knowing how to execute them in the real world."

A slow smile curved the edges of Payton's lips. She could never say no to a challenge.

Against her better judgment and the threat of ruining one of her best pairs of panty hose, Payton kicked her heels off and tossed the ball to Cedric. She jogged a few yards away, turned and caught his light pass with minimal effort.

"You throw like a girl," Payton taunted.

"Maybe because I'm throwing *to* a girl?"

"Well, try to forget that detail," she said, throwing the ball back to him with a lot more force than he'd used.

He caught the ball against his chest. "I told you once before, there's no way I can miss the fact that you're all woman."

A tingle traveled up Payton's spine, just like the first time he'd said those words to her.

"Ready?" Cedric called, his arm poised to throw.

"Hold on," she said. She jogged to the other end of the room. "I want to see if they've got you playing the right position." She held out her hands. "Ready."

The ball came spiraling toward her. Payton reached up and caught it midair. She tucked the ball between her arm and chest, just as her daddy had taught his players, then she took off toward an invisible goal on the other side of the room.

Cedric waited for her, crouched like a defender, a wide smile spread across that gorgeous face.

Payton tried to sidestep him, but he caught her from behind, his arms locking around her waist.

"Hey!" she protested. "I thought this was supposed to be *touch* football?"

"Exactly," he whispered against her neck. His hold tightened, his strong hands spanning her waist, his fingers inches from her breasts. Before she could utter a protest, Cedric's lips connected with the one spot on her neck that drove her mindless.

Payton gasped with need, covering the arms that latched around her and throwing her head back to give him better access. Still locked together, Cedric shuffled them to the wall. He turned her around and pinned her against it, then zeroed in on her neck again, kissing and licking and nipping his way up and down.

He found her breast. Despite the layers of clothing separating his hand and her skin, her body's reaction couldn't have been stronger if they were both naked. Her nipple puckered, instantly drawing tight. Her skin burned from the inside out.

Cedric released her neck from his erotic assault. His hand continued to caress her breast as he stared into her eyes, seeking permission. With a slight nod, Payton put an end to both their miseries. Permission granted.

He lowered his head and captured her mouth, trailing his tongue along her lips, applying just enough pressure to coax them open. As soon as Payton relinquished, his tongue plunged into her mouth, thrusting with a power that electrified her. He fisted his left hand in her hair, his right hand still on her breast, squeezing, caressing, driving her out of her mind.

A moan escaped her throat. It only encouraged him

to kiss her harder, deeper. Payton ran her hands up and down his back, bunching the wet T-shirt in her fist. She hiked her skirt up to the tops of her thighs and wrapped her right leg around him, clutching him to her.

The sound of a car door slamming knocked Payton out of the sensual fairy tale she'd fallen into.

"Cedric, stop!" She used both hands to push at his chest.

He backed away, his labored breaths soughing in and out of his mouth. He looked dazed and confused, exactly how she felt at the moment. It was hard to think. She couldn't concentrate on anything with the sparks of electricity still firing from a thousand different points on her body.

"Sorry that took so long," Mrs. Shipley called. "You get a little bit of rain and traffic comes to a standstill."

Payton quickly pulled her suit jacket closed to cover the damp spots Cedric's wet T-shirt had made on her satin shell. She turned to Mrs. Shipley, hoping the flush had faded from her cheeks.

"So," Mrs. Shipley said, looking from Payton to Cedric. "Should we discuss today?"

"Cedric has to leave," Payton abruptly announced.

Cedric's eyes darted to her. His jaw drew as hard as stone, but he didn't refute her hastily fabricated claim.

The center's director turned to Cedric with hands outstretched. She grabbed his palm for an enthusiastic handshake. "Thank you so much for today. The kids will talk about this all year."

"It was my pleasure," he answered. Then his eyes flashed back to Payton. He didn't say anything, just stared at her for a moment before inclining his head and heading for the door. He stopped in the middle of the center and retrieved the mesh bag with the uniform equipment and said over his shoulder, "Keep the footballs for the kids."

With that, he exited the center, leaving Payton with an ache in her chest and a fire still burning in her belly.

## Chapter 9

Cedric gripped the edge of the bathroom counter and raised his head. He stared into the mirror, studying his reflection, doing his damnedest to make sure no evidence of the riot going on inside his head showed on his face.

If tonight didn't kill him, he could get through anything.

A couple of days ago, when he'd invited Payton to accompany him to Torrian and Paige's engagement party, it had been mostly about business. He knew the place would be wall-to-wall with industry professionals who would be more interested in talking football than celebrating the happy couple's pending nuptials.

What Cedric had not anticipated was seeing Payton outside of her normal work mode. Gone was the briefcase and restricting business suit. Tonight she wore a seductive little black dress that hugged every curve and stopped just above her knees. After feeling those curves pressed up against him earlier today, all he could think about tonight was getting close to her.

When Payton had opened her front door in that silky, sexy dress, Cedric's first instinct was to say to hell with the party and sequester them in her apartment. But one kiss—as unbelievable as it was—didn't give him the right to expect anything more from her. And now he was forced to spend hours with her at this party, knowing what her lips felt like, how her mouth tasted, how her breasts felt inside his palm and against his chest.

And he couldn't do a damn thing about it.

The door opened and his temporary sanctuary was instantly imbued with the noisy chatter that filtered in from the party. Torrian entered the bathroom, followed by Jared.

"Hey, you hiding out on us?" Torrian asked.

"Just taking a break," Cedric answered. "It's packed out there."

"This is the place to be tonight," Jared said. He clamped a hand on Torrian's shoulder. "I think most people are still trying to figure out how you and Paige hooked up after that knock-down, drag-out fight you two had on her blog."

Torrian had met his future wife, local entertainment writer Paige Turner, after she'd trashed his new book in a review on her blog. The fallout from their online squabble and a cooking competition the two had participated in on a local morning news show had kept all of New York glued to the television.

"Most of the people out there couldn't care less that Paige and I are getting married. Other than a few family members and friends, the guest list was pure strategy on Paige's part," Torrian said. "That woman is always working some angle. She has every food critic in the city out there."

"She's a businesswoman." Jared shrugged. "This restaurant is now her business."

"And business has skyrocketed since she took over the restaurant's marketing and PR. My future wife is definitely a savvy businesswoman. And speaking of businesswomen," Torrian said, stepping up to a urinal. "That agent of yours is working the room. I told my agent he'd better watch out. Payton may steal some of his clients right out from under him."

"Especially the way she's looking tonight in that dress," Jared said.

Cedric took a step toward Jared, his right hand clenched into a fist. "What did I tell you about looking at my agent that way?"

Jared backed away, his hands held up in mock surrender. "Damn, man, would you chill? Learn how to take a joke. Remember I have a girlfriend out there. I'm not about to step out on Samantha," Jared said, turning toward the wall of urinals.

Cedric unclenched his fist and took a deep breath.

Torrian washed his hands, then leaned a hip against the sink, his arms crossed over his chest.

"What?" Cedric asked, knowing Torrian had something to say. Torrian always had something to say.

"Are you sure you want to go there with Payton?" his former teammate asked.

"I don't know what you're talking about," Cedric said. His reply sounded like bull even to his own ears.

"Don't play dumb. You need to keep this thing strictly about business. Don't blur the lines, Ced. It'll only lead to trouble."

"There are no blurry lines, all right?" Cedric said.

He attempted to move past him, but Torrian caught him on the shoulder.

"You sure about that?" Torrian asked. "We used to trash Gus Houseman and you never gave a damn. Now you're ready to tear Jared's head off because he mentioned Payton's dress? This isn't smart, Cedric. There's a reason old sayings become old sayings, and 'don't mix business with pleasure' is one of the oldest in the book. Think about it, man."

Cedric knew Torrian was right. Hell, hadn't he been telling himself the same thing for the past few weeks? He needed to concentrate on his career and making sure he remained a member of the Sabers's organization. Derek was counting on him, and there was nothing more important than making sure his brother had everything he needed, including having Cedric only an hour's drive away. Nothing else should matter.

But there was a short circuit between the rational part of his brain and the part that took one look at Payton and wanted to strip her clothes off and pin her against the nearest wall. He closed his eyes against the image that thought created but it only intensified in his imagination.

God, this was *killing* him.

Cedric opened his eyes and found Jared and Torrian both staring at him.

Jared shook his head, a grin hitching up the corner of his mouth. "You've got it bad, man."

Cedric groaned. If it was evident to these two, then everybody could probably see just how bad he really *did* have it for his agent. How could he offer Payton discretion if his feelings were so transparent?

"So what do I do?" he asked them both.

"Don't ask me," Torrian said. "You're at my engagement party, remember?"

"Can't help you either, man. I'll be the first to admit Samantha's got me eating out of the palm of her hand," Jared said, clapping a hand on Cedric's back as the three of them exited the restroom.

As they rejoined the party, Cedric had a feeling his situation was beyond help. When he spotted Payton standing with a circle of other women, including Paige and Deirdre Smallwood, Torrian's sister, he knew it for certain.

He was in major trouble.

Payton's head flew back as she laughed, and his eyes were immediately drawn to her neck. Just like that, Cedric was right back to their kiss that afternoon. He could feel her soft skin on his lips, taste her sweet flavor on his tongue. Every time he looked at her, his mind conjured images of what they had done in that rec center, and everything he'd wanted to do. Everything he *still* wanted to do.

His groin tightened at the thought, and Cedric knew he wouldn't be satisfied until he got the chance to explore every single inch of her.

Tonight would be damn near impossible to endure. And he had a feeling it was going to get more difficult every minute they were around each other.

Payton told herself to slow down. She had never been one to overindulge, usually stopping after one or two drinks. But she was having such a great time and the champagne and wine from the Fire Starter Grille's extensive collection was flowing as freely as a creek in springtime.

The night had been so festive it was hard not to get

into the spirit. Everything had been over the top, starting with the delicious six-course meal they had been treated to, which had been punctuated by various toasts from friends and family members of the couple, along with a host of Sabers players.

What a difference a few weeks made. She had spent months just trying to get close enough to introduce herself to many of these players. And here she was, rubbing elbows with them and being her most charming. At least Payton hoped she was being charming. After her third glass of champagne, everything out of her mouth seemed witty.

"Are you having a good time?" a deep voice asked from just beyond her shoulder.

Payton spun around, her elbow crashing into Cedric's chest. The champagne jostled in her glass and she wobbled slightly. Cedric caught her arm and helped to steady her. She decided then and there to cut herself off. Tonight's champagne, along with all the wine she'd consumed with her meal, was more alcohol than she usually drank in an entire month. She placed her nearly full champagne flute on a nearby table and turned fully to face Cedric.

"I'm having a great time," she answered with the enthusiastic slur of the slightly tipsy. "A little *too* great, maybe."

Payton could feel the blush creep up her cheeks. Or maybe she had been blushing all along and it had only intensified now that Cedric was near. Champagne had that effect on her and, Lord knows, so did Cedric.

"Good," he said, grabbing another glass of champagne from a passing waiter and wrapping her fingers around the stem. "You've been working hard this past month. You deserve to celebrate a bit."

He was right. She had been working nonstop since the moment he'd signed on as her client. This was her first chance to step back and enjoy herself.

"You sure picked a great spot," she said, motioning to their surroundings. The Fire Starter Grille, the brainchild of Torrian Smallwood, was the hottest new restaurant in central Manhattan, and Torrian's sister Deirdre, the head chef, was making waves on the culinary scene. Payton had never even tried getting a reservation here. It was a well-known fact that the waiting list was months long.

"Torrian does throw a great party," Cedric agreed. "Have you been making the most of the situation?" he asked.

"If you mean shoving my business card at every football player in the room, then, no, I haven't," she said. "I've introduced myself to a few players I've been eyeing, but nothing more."

"That's part of the reason I brought you here, Payton. To make connections. You have every right to look for new clients," he said. "I don't expect to be the only player on your roster."

"And hopefully you won't. But I still have to prove myself to a lot of people before other athletes believe I'm the real deal. That's why I'm concentrating on making your career everything it should be. You're going to get one hundred percent of me."

"Is that a promise?" he asked.

The husky timbre of his voice, combined with the smoldering look in his eyes, told Payton they were no longer talking about contract negotiations. Instead of answering his question she downed the remaining champagne in one gulp, though it did nothing to cool the raging inferno in her belly.

The beginning chords of Roberta Flack's version of

"Killing Me Softly with His Song" trickled from the speakers that were so discretely placed around the room Payton had yet to actually spot one.

"Oh." She brought her hand to her chest. "I haven't heard this in years," she said. "This was the song my mom and dad danced to at their wedding, and whenever it came on the radio, they always stopped whatever they were doing so they could dance. It didn't matter if they were at home, out with company, even driving."

"Driving?"

"That's right," Payton nodded. "Dad would pull onto the shoulder of the road and they would dance." Payton wrapped her arms around herself, soaking in the memory.

Cedric placed the champagne he'd been sipping onto a nearby table. "That sounds like a tradition worth carrying on." He held out his hand. "May I have this dance?"

Payton's heart constricted. An emotion she could hardly describe lodged itself so firmly in her throat she couldn't speak. Instead, she placed her hand in the cradle of Cedric's warm palm.

He pulled her in close, entwining the fingers of his right hand with hers while his left settled against the small of her back. The spot where he touched tingled, radiating warmth throughout her entire body. As they swayed back and forth to the familiar tune, all Payton could think about was how right this felt, even while another part of her brain knew it was wrong.

No, not wrong, just unwise. Nothing that felt this good could be completely wrong.

She rested her cheek against his shoulder, marveling at the strength of the muscle. "You feel so good," she whispered.

"Not as good as you feel," he replied so softly Payton could barely hear it. He increased the pressure on her back, pulling her in closer contact with the solid wall of his body. There was no mistaking the arousal pressing against her stomach, and the power she felt there had the same heady effect as the alcohol she'd consumed tonight.

"Are you ready to leave?" Cedric asked.

She raised her head, her eyes meeting his. The champagne had certainly elicited a compelling buzz, but Payton wasn't so tipsy that she could misinterpret what she saw staring back at her.

Desire.

Raw and potent. Hot and heart-stopping.

It so closely mirrored what she had been feeling ever since their kiss that afternoon, she was sure Cedric could see right through her.

"Yes," she finally answered.

The look in Cedric's eyes became even more smoldering. Payton knew anyone paying attention would clearly recognize what was transpiring between them. This was a foolish mistake, blatantly engaging in what amounted to public foreplay with her client. But for the life of her Payton could not tear her gaze away from Cedric's stare and the frank, honest desire she found there.

Without so much as a farewell wish to the hosts, they left the party.

The thirty-minute drive from midtown Manhattan to her apartment was completed in silence, but the sexual tension suffusing the tight confines of the vehicle said more than either of them could have verbalized. As Cedric helped her out of his SUV, Payton's breasts grazed his chest. She felt his swift intake of breath and realized he was wound as tightly as she was.

With his hand lightly touching the small of her back, Cedric guided her to her apartment.

Payton's hands fumbled with the key a few times before she was finally able to unlock the door.

"I'll follow you in, just to make sure you're safe," Cedric said.

"I'd like that," Payton replied. She wobbled slightly. She'd definitely had too much to drink if the champagne was still affecting her so much. Though, to be honest, the tremble in her limbs had just as much to do with the man standing only inches behind her.

She entered the apartment first, flicking on the lamp that sat on a table next to the door. She tossed her keys onto the wooden tray next to it, then turned to Cedric, who stood just inside the open door.

Payton stretched a hand toward him, then beyond, to the door, shutting it and pushing him back against it. As soon as the door shut, Cedric caught her head between his palms and captured her mouth in an eager assault of lips, teeth and tongue. Payton's blood rushed through her veins as his insistent tongue plunged and retreated, emulating a rhythm that sent shockwaves directly to the spot pulsing between her thighs.

"God, you taste good," he murmured.

Payton couldn't speak. This full-blown attack on her sensory system made it hard to concentrate on anything else. In and out his tongue dipped, dancing with her own. He swirled it around, caressing the inside of her mouth.

Cedric's hands began a slow journey from her face, along her arms, stopping at her backside where he clutched her and pulled her against his body. The thickness of the arousal straining against her stomach caused all manner of deliciously illicit thoughts to flutter through her brain. Payton undulated against him, wrangling a moan from deep within Cedric's throat. His hands gripped her ass harder, pulling her more snuggly to his rock-hard body.

Payton melted against him, her limbs losing all control. When Cedric's right hand dipped underneath the hem of her short black dress, a tiny alarm sounded in her brain, but Payton silenced it. Her body needed this. She would deal with the consequences later.

As his tongue continued to explore her mouth, Cedric's fingers began a new journey along her body. Moving her satin thong to the side, he glided a single strong finger from front to back, drawing moisture from her core. With exquisite expertise he teased the bundle of nerves at her center into a tight ball before plunging a single, thick finger into her.

Payton cried out as her body stretched around his finger, clutching it as it pushed deeper and deeper. It retreated, then pushed in again, sinking farther and higher with every thrust. Payton's entire being seized as wicked pleasure cascaded throughout her bloodstream. She came hard and fast, clutching Cedric's shoulders, burying her head against his chest. She held on to him for all she was worth, her trembling limbs worthless as sparks of sensation continually shot through her body.

"Oh, my God," Payton breathed. She sucked in air like a drowning woman, hoping the oxygen would clear her brain enough to concentrate on something other than the orgasm she was still trying to hold on to.

"That was…uh…nice," she said.

"You're welcome," Cedric whispered into her ear. Testing her legs, she concluded she could walk without melting onto the floor in a puddle of satisfied woman. She captured Cedric's hand and tugged, starting toward her bedroom, but he pulled away.

He banged his head against the door, clenching his eyes tight.

"What's wrong?" Payton asked, reaching again for his hand.

"Nothing," he said. "Just kicking myself."

"Why?"

"Because I'm about to do the hardest thing I've ever done," he answered.

Payton stared at him, confusion mixing with the lingering effects of the alcohol and orgasm to create a bewilderment her muddled brain was far too tired to figure out. She didn't want to think too much.

"We can't do this tonight, Payton."

Protests rang throughout her brain. She clasped her hands around his head and tried to pull him in for another kiss, but he captured her forearms in a gentle but firm grip. He pulled her arms to her sides, leaned in and kissed her forehead.

"If we go through with this tonight, you're going to wake up tomorrow morning regretting the hell out of it. I can't let that happen." He pressed his forehead against hers and stared into her eyes. "When we do make love, I want to know it's because you want to be with me, not because you had too much champagne."

The disappointment that had consumed her since he'd halted their kiss had been replaced by something much more profound. Gratitude. That he was enough of a gentleman not to take advantage of her when she was literally handing herself to him on a golden platter spoke volumes even to her inebriated brain.

Cedric took her by the hand and gently prodded her

toward her bedroom. Once there, he sat her on the bed. Payton's hands went to the hem of her dress, but he halted her movement.

"Wait until I leave. I can only take so much."

"Sorry," she murmured, contrite.

She didn't move a muscle until her bedroom door clicked. When it did, Payton was too tired to do anything but fall onto her pillow.

When she awoke the next morning, she was still in her favorite black cocktail dress. Foundation was smeared against her beige pillowcase, and her head felt as if every marching band in the Macy's Thanksgiving Day Parade was serenading her. All at the same time.

Coffee. She needed coffee now.

Payton took a deep breath and decided she needed a toothbrush even more. She stumbled into the bathroom and scrubbed the remaining makeup from her face before brushing her teeth and pulling a brush through her hair. She stared into the mirror, shaking her head in shame at the image staring back at her.

What had she done last night?

Unfortunately, the morning's hangover didn't include memory loss. No, she remembered every minute of it. The wine and champagne she'd overindulged in. The way she'd thrown herself at Cedric.

The orgasm he'd given her.

She clutched the edges of her pedestal sink as her body trembled involuntarily at the memory. If they had gone through with what she'd wanted last night it would have been disastrous on so many levels. But it also would have been phenomenal. She knew that with every trembling fiber of her body.

"Forget last night," Payton told the rumpled woman staring back at her.

She peeled out of her black dress and pulled on a robe. Before she showered she needed to get some caffeine flowing through her system. She headed for the kitchen, but the massive helping of male sprawled on her living room sofa stopped her dead in her tracks.

Cedric lay with one hand behind his head, the other atop his flat washboard stomach, which was covered only by a thin undershirt beneath his unbuttoned shirt. He'd kicked his shoes off and unzipped his black pants.

Payton tiptoed to the hallway linen closet, but when she returned with the crocheted blanket her mother had given her for her high school graduation, Cedric's eyes were staring back at her.

"I was going to cover you," she said unnecessarily. She was in serious inward-cringe mode. It had been a long time since she'd done the awkward morning-after routine, and they hadn't even gone all the way last night.

Thank God.

He pushed himself up and made room for her on the sofa. Self-preservation demanded she stay right where she was, but Payton took the seat next to him anyway.

He sat with his elbows resting on his knees, his clamped hands hanging between them. His head was bowed and Payton could see the tension in his shoulders.

"Thank you for stopping me last night," she said. When she thought about the disaster sleeping with him would have created, Payton wanted to bury her head back into the pillow. Yet her body still mourned the pleasure she knew Cedric would have given her.

"That's not what I meant to do last night," he said.

"You…what?" Payton asked.

He looked at her. "I wasn't stopping anything. Just postponing the inevitable."

"Cedric—"

"Don't sit there and tell me you don't want me, Payton. If you try I'll remind you of every moan that came out of your mouth last night."

"Cedric, please."

"The only thing that stopped me was the fact that you'd had too much to drink. But you're awake and sober this morning and I want to throw you on this sofa and bury myself inside you more than I want to take my next breath."

Payton nearly orgasmed then and there.

She'd never gone for the alpha types, but the force of Cedric's words did things to her she was ashamed to admit. How was she supposed to function around him, knowing what he wanted to do to her? What she wanted him to do to her. And she *did* want it. Desperately.

"We can't," she said, hating the words, but knowing they needed to be spoken. "It would compromise everything."

"It's already compromised us, Payton. Do you think I can look at you and not remember the way you came around my fingers last night? From this point on, that's the first thing I'll think about when I see you. And you'll know it's what I'm thinking about."

Pleasure rippled through her. She squeezed her legs together and swallowed the moan that nearly escaped her throat.

"One time," he said in an achingly gentle voice. "Can't we just go there one time and get it out of our systems?"

"Would one time be enough?" Payton returned, knowing the answer before she even asked the question.

One time would never be enough for her. "I'll admit that I want you," she said. "But…"

Cedric shot up from the sofa and ran both hands over his head and down his face. He turned to her, and the desperation on his face caused an ache to settle deep within her chest.

"This has gone way past me just wanting you, Payton. I *need* you."

"Oh, God," she groaned. Cradling her head in her hands, she massaged her temples, wishing she could take back the past twenty-four hours. She knew things were heading this way between them, but she'd had a handle on it. If not for the kiss at that rec center yesterday, or all the alcohol she'd drank last night.

If she hadn't let him bring her to orgasm right in this very room.

"Oh, *God*," she groaned louder, giving in to the urge to bury her head in the throw pillow on her sofa.

"That's not the response I was hoping for," Cedric said in a velvety voice.

Payton's shoulders tensed as he covered them with his hands. She opened her eyes to find him crouched in front of her, his penetrating stare aiming straight to the heart of her. He captured her chin in his fingers and leaned forward, brushing his lips against hers. With gentle insistence, he urged her mouth open, pushing his tongue inside.

With a soft cry, Payton closed her eyes and accepted her fate.

She slipped her hand around the back of his head and clasped him to her, meeting his tongue stroke for stroke as he bathed the inside of her mouth with hungry, mind-numbing kisses. She ran her other hand down his back, marveling in the strength of the well-honed muscles undulating against her fingertips.

And when Cedric turned slightly and slanted over her, Payton followed his lead, reclining on the sofa and pulling him on top of her. He quickly got rid of his shirt, then swooped down and reclaimed her mouth. His hand snaked down her torso, unbelting her terrycloth robe. He ran his palm across her bare stomach, then inched lower, tunneling past the rim of her lace panties and delving into the moist spot between her thighs. He slid his tongue along the edge of her demi bra, then drew it across her nipple, lapping at the taut peak through the lacy fabric.

Payton melted against his fingers, mewling in satisfaction as he teased her clitoris into an erect, pulsing bud of sensation. He massaged the nub with his thumb as he slid first one and then a second finger inside her. Payton clinched around him, pushing her hips higher, trying to get his fingers as deep as they could go.

"Cedric, please," she begged, needing to come with a ferocity that had her mindless with want. He gave her what she needed, pumping his fingers in and out with rapid strokes as he took her aching nipple in his mouth and sucked her hard through the fabric. Payton clamped her hands around his head and held his mouth in place as she shuddered around his fingers.

She collapsed back on the sofa, her limbs liquefied after the shattering release.

"Don't you fall asleep," came Cedric's silky warning. "We're just getting started."

He pressed his mouth to her stomach and peppered her skin with kisses, licking his way around her waist as he caught the edge of her panties and pulled them down her legs. Payton heard him emit a low groan, then she gasped with pleasure as he pressed a swift, decadent kiss against her soaking wet sex.

He pushed himself up and hooked his thumbs into his waistband, shoving his pants and boxers past his hips. He picked his wallet up from the floor, pulled out a condom, and swiftly rolled it over his erection. Then he reached over and captured her by the waist.

Pulling her onto his lap so that she straddled his thighs, he ran his tongue along her collarbone. Then with both hands grasping her hips, he guided her onto his erection.

Payton's back bowed as she lowered herself, taking him inside of her. Inch by glorious inch, he invaded her body, stretching her to the limit with his thick, hard flesh. Payton clamped both hands on his shoulders as she lifted herself up and down the length of him, marveling in each decadent stroke.

Cedric leaned forward and sucked one nipple into his mouth, then switched to the other, teasing the rigid points with his teeth and tongue. With his hands, he directed her movements as she rocked against him, lifting her up his long, solid shaft, then guiding her down. Down, down, down. Until she was completely impaled.

The tempo of her strokes increased as she began to pump faster and faster. She sank her fingers into his shoulders and rode him hard, pounding against his thighs as he drove himself hot and hard inside of her.

Payton shattered around him, her body convulsing as she was hit with wave upon wave of erotic pleasure. She collapsed against Cedric's chest, her breath coming in labored pants.

She lay upon his sweat-slicked chest, completely spent. Yet before her body could even start to recover from the mind-shattering ride he'd just taken her on, her brain began to assault her with the repercussions of what she'd done.

Shame washed over her.

There were strict lines that she could not cross, and sleeping with her client was one of them. At least she had the excuse of being too inebriated last night. She didn't have any excuses today. There was no way to justify what had just happened here.

She levered herself up and tried to climb down from his waist, but he gripped her hips and held her in place.

"Don't," he said.

"Cedric, please let go," Payton begged.

"*No.* Dammit, Payton. Don't start regretting this already."

She peeled his hands from her hips and lifted herself off of his lap, grabbing her robe and quickly putting it on. She cinched the belt at her waist and scooted to the opposite end of the couch, resting her elbows on her knees and cradling her face in her hands.

"This was a mistake," she whispered.

She heard his low curse as he pushed himself up from the sofa, then the rustling of his pants as he pulled them up from where they'd pooled at his feet.

Payton took a deep breath and said, "I'm sorry."

"Just stop talking, all right? If the only thing you have to say after having sex with me is 'I'm sorry' and 'it was a mistake,' just don't say anything."

"I explained from the very beginning—"

"Yeah, I know. 'Strictly professional.' Well, what we just did shoots that rule to hell, Payton. We can't do strictly professional."

"We have to," she said. Payton took a deep, fortifying

breath. "I know normally this would make things awkward, but we're both adults. We can make the decision right now to put this incident behind us."

"Incident?"

The hurt in that single word sliced through her. Payton pushed a shaking hand through her hair.

"I don't mean to downplay what went on here," she said. "But we need to bury this, Cedric. Please, for both our sakes, just forget it ever happened."

"Don't even try to tell me to forget what just happened," he warned with a vicious hiss. He shook his head and planted his hands on his hips. "I just don't get it."

"Get what?" she asked, trying not to stare at the fly of his black trousers that was still halfway unzipped. Instead she concentrated on the gold watch peeking out from under the cuff of his tailored shirt. "What don't you get?"

"How you can respond the way you did a few minutes ago and now pretend it means nothing."

Payton brought her eyes back to his, understanding the frustration she found there. She was experiencing it too, along with about a million other emotions. They were both to blame for the position they were now in, even though the ground rules had been clearly set when they first started working together.

Well, she was not going to allow things to go further.

Payton sat up straight, shoring up her defenses.

"I never said it meant nothing, Cedric, but my career means more. It has to. I've sacrificed too much to get to this point and I refuse to throw it all away for sex."

The look in his eyes was so hard, so intense. When he finally spoke his voice was as hard as his eyes. "If all I wanted from you is sex I never would have stopped us last night. I would have taken what you pushed in my face and been out of here before you ever woke up."

He stood before her, his arms crossed over his chest. "You don't get it, do you? I don't want just sex, Payton. I want *you*."

Payton dropped her head. Her chest was so tight she could hardly breathe.

"You can't have me," she finally answered. "Not in that way. As your agent, you get one hundred percent of me. But that's all I can give you, Cedric."

Without another word, Cedric reached over and grabbed the tailored jacket he'd draped across the arm of the sofa. Her eyes firmly planted on the floor, Payton saw him slip into a pair of loafers. She hoped he would slam the door so she'd have something to blame him for, but he wouldn't give her even that much. Slipping quietly out of her apartment, he softly shut the door behind him.

Payton grabbed a throw pillow and hugged it to her chest, trying to swallow past the boulder-size lump lodged in her throat.

This was for the best.

Payton knew she'd done what she'd had to do. Maybe if she repeated it enough, she could convince her heart to believe it.

# Chapter 10

"Dude, would you pay attention?"

A wadded paper napkin bounced off the side of Cedric's head.

"What?" he groused, scooping up the napkin and pitching it back at Torrian.

"It's your play," Torrian said. "Again."

"Yeah, hurry it up, Ced," Jared added. "With that extra morning practice coach ordered I only have another twenty minutes before I need to hit the sack." He turned to Torrian. "You couldn't talk the coach out of that?"

"I'm the one who suggested it," Torrian replied. "The Bears always give us trouble, especially in their own stadium. The team needs the extra practice."

"Maybe your wide receivers do," Jared said. "The guys on Special Teams have been kicking ass lately. So has my man here. You lit up the field against San Diego, man. Cedric?"

"What?" Cedric asked again.

"What the hell is up with you?" Jared glared at him. "You've been acting as if someone ran over your dog or something."

Cedric shrugged. "We're nearing the end of the regular season. Everybody's wound tight now that the playoffs are in our sights."

"We've gone to the playoffs every year since you joined the team." Torrian slapped the table they'd commandeered in one of the hotel's meeting rooms, indicating he wanted another card. "I've never seen you this quiet."

"I come up for contract renewal at the end of the season," Cedric tried. "I've got a lot on my mind." He hoped Torrian would leave it alone. He should have known better.

"You know what I think?" Torrian asked.

"The question is do I *care* what you think. The answer is no." Cedric took a pull on his beer, not even tasting the icy liquid.

"I think this has something to do with you leaving my engagement party last Saturday night with your agent. Don't think no one noticed."

"I hadn't noticed." Jared's brows peaked. "Man, did you hit that?"

"Shut the hell up," Cedric shot at him.

"What?" Jared held his hands up, the innocent victim. "That would be a good thing, wouldn't it? You know… woman…sex? That's good, right?" he asked Torrian.

"Payton is my agent," Cedric said, staring at the pair of queens in his hand. "Have you slept with your agent?"

"Besides the fact that he's a dude," Jared drawled, "he's also married. I don't break up happy families."

Cedric doubted he'd ever wanted to murder someone more than he wanted to kill his teammate right now. "My relationship with my agent is no different than anyone else's. It's business, period."

"I don't get why you would sign with a woman agent if you're not going to try to get with her," Jared said.

God, did this guy not know when to let things drop?

"You can be such an idiot," Torrian said.

"Thank you," Cedric agreed.

"I was talking to you," Torrian threw his way.

"Me?" His brows shot up. "How am I the idiot here? Weren't you the one who told me I shouldn't mix business with pleasure?"

"That's when I thought you just wanted to get a little something on the side. It's obviously more than that or your head wouldn't be so messed up."

"There's nothing wrong with my head."

Jared pointed at him. "Actually—"

"Shut up." He cut off whatever asinine nonsense Jared was about to spew. "Payton is my agent," he stated again. "Nothing more."

Despite the knot that formed in his stomach every time he thought about the morning he'd walked out of her apartment, Cedric was starting to accept that Payton had been right to send him away. She was his agent, a business partner he'd hired for the sole purpose of furthering his career. Even though he'd tried to tell himself that their sleeping together wouldn't muddy the waters of their professional relationship, things had already changed. He hadn't talked to her in days. How could they work together if they couldn't even talk to each other?

He needed Payton as his agent more than he needed her in his bed. That point had been brought home with a call on Tuesday from the director of Marshall's Place telling him that Derek had fallen and suffered a sprain during one of his physical therapy sessions. Even though Mrs. Bea had assured him that Derek was doing well, Cedric had still rushed to the facility, needing to see for himself that his brother was indeed okay.

If he were playing in Arizona or Los Angeles or Miami, getting to Derek so quickly wouldn't have been possible. He had to remain in New York. Nothing could get in the way of his ultimate goal: securing a new long-term contract with the Sabers so he could remain close to his brother.

"I fold." Jared tossed his cards down and pushed his chair away from the table. "It's time for me to bail. I told Samantha I would call her before I hit the sack."

"I'm done, too," Torrian said, looking at his cell phone. "Paige is on her way up to the room, and I'd much rather look at her face than your ugly mugs."

"Whatever." Jared punched him playfully on the arm. "You heading up, Ced?"

"Soon," Cedric replied. "I'll catch you guys in the morning."

As he watched his friends leave, Cedric couldn't help the twinge of regret that hit his chest dead center. Jared and his girlfriend Samantha had been together since college. Torrian and Paige, who'd started out as enemies, were now the poster children for happy couples.

He wanted what his friends had. He wanted someone to call and wish good night. Someone waiting for him when he came back from road games like this one, or who would even join him on the road the way Paige had joined Torrian here in Chicago.

As they did so often, thoughts of Payton bombarded him. How easily he could envision her by his side, as so much more than just his agent. Images of her face as she came apart in his arms flooded his mind. Would he ever be able to erase that vision? He doubted it. Every moan she'd made was etched into his memory.

But that's all he would ever have. Memories.

Payton had made her wishes loud and clear. There would be nothing more between them. He'd had years of being "just a client" to Gus. He knew the drill. If that's how she wanted it, that's what she would get.


Payton grazed her thumb over the smooth keys of her BlackBerry. She'd been staring at it for the past five minutes, debating whether to send an email or pull on her big girl panties and actually make a call. She hadn't spoken to Cedric in nearly three weeks. The few exchanges they'd had had been conducted solely through email or text message.

It helped that the Sabers had a stretch of three road games. He was always harder to pin down when he was on the road. It was easier to just shoot him a message and await his response. At least that's the excuse that sounded the best to her ears.

In truth, Payton couldn't bear to hear his voice that first week after. *After* needed no qualification. She would always think of that morning when he'd left her sitting on her sofa as *after*.

But text messages and email were out of the question today. Following the excited call from her mother last night and the special favor she'd requested, Payton knew an email to Cedric would not suffice. She needed to hear the inflection in his voice so she could try to gauge the meaning behind his answer, whatever the answer might be.

Her decision made, she took a sip of her chai latte—her second of the day—and glanced around her makeshift office. The first thing she would do with her commission from the Soft Touch Shaving Cream deal was invest in an office with more privacy than back tables at coffee shops. Making confidential calls surrounded by strangers was *so* not her thing.

Payton clicked through the electronic address book until she found Cedric's number and hit send before she could stop herself. As the phone trilled in her ear, she sucked in a couple of fortifying breaths and reminded herself that she was a grown woman. There was no reason to feel anxious.

"Reeves," he answered after five rings.

Some of the air from her balloon of confidence deflated at Cedric's impersonal greeting. No doubt he'd recognized her number on his screen, yet he'd answered the phone as if speaking to a stranger.

Or a business partner.

"Hello, Cedric," Payton answered. "Good game yesterday."

Strict. Professional. Very agent-like.

"Thanks," he said, clipped.

As silence stretched between them Payton wasn't sure which she'd rather be doing right now, getting a root canal or banging her head against a brick wall. Either seemed more enjoyable than what could only be described as the most awkward conversation in the world. The best way to bring an end to this torture was to just say what she needed to say and be done with it.

"I have a favor to ask of you," she continued. "My mother called last night. The school board has decided to rename the football stadium at my old high school in honor of my dad." She paused. When there was no response, Payton soldiered on. "There's a banquet this Thursday and a dedication ceremony at the game this Friday night. Since my dad really admired you as a player, my mother was hoping you could attend the ceremony. It would be a huge deal to have a real NFL player there."

With each passing second her anxiety multiplied. Just as Payton was about to tell him to forget she'd asked, Cedric's stoic voice broke through the silence.

"What time does our plane leave?"

That was it? Just like that he was on board?

"I…uh, I haven't searched for flights yet. I'll do so this afternoon and get back to you."

"Just book me on whatever flight you're on. I have to be back in New York Saturday afternoon to fly out with the team to Baltimore."

"Yes, I know," she said. After a pause, she added a heartfelt "Thank you, Cedric."

"I'll see you Thursday," he said before disconnecting the call.

What had just happened there?

The better question was what *hadn't* happened. No teasing. No banter. Not even a minute of the comfortable small talk she and Cedric had shared from the first moment they'd met. Payton understood the message he was trying to send. He was giving her what she'd asked for, a strictly professional relationship between agent and client. But his clipped words and icy tone were taking it to the extreme. They had to have some kind of rapport if they were going to continue working together.

The urge to rewind life's clock struck her again, as it had way too many times over the past few weeks. If only they could go back to when she'd first signed him as a client, she would do things differently.

At least as far as their personal relationship was concerned.

On the professional front, Payton had surprised herself with all she'd accomplished in these two short months. She'd landed him a respectable endorsement deal and was very close to securing another with ES Gaming. Depending on his rushing yardage at the end of the season, which was already nearing a Sabers single-season record, Cedric might even land the coveted spot on the cover of the company's latest football video game.

She had done a phenomenal job as his agent, and others were taking notice. She'd had two calls from Sabers players who were thinking of switching agents. Things were looking up for Mosely Sports Management.

So why did she have this hollowed-out feeling in her chest?

This was everything she'd wanted, wasn't it? It was why she'd quit the law firm and stepped out on faith that sports agenting was what she was meant to do with her life.

Payton clicked on the "missed calls" icon on her cell phone and scrolled through the list. Daniel McNamara had called her on Sunday afternoon. Payton had deliberately let the call go to voice mail, but Daniel's quick "just checking in on you" message had left much to interpretation. His offer from several weeks ago to make her a partner and the head of the law firm's huge negotiations division had come back to taunt—or better yet, haunt—her often over the past month.

In the beginning it had been easy to brush the idea off without much afterthought, but as time passed, other thoughts began to take root. The peace of mind that came with a steady paycheck every month. The prestige of being named partner—the first African American woman to garner that distinction in the law firm's nearly fifty-year history.

But there was another side to the coin. Even though she would technically supervise nearly a hundred associates, she would no longer be her own boss. She would still have to answer to the partners. And as one of the youngest, newest division heads, she would be viewed as the untested rookie among upper management.

One of the most alluring advantages to accepting Daniel's offer was the one that made Payton inwardly cringe with the most shame. If she gave up being a sports agent and went back to practicing law, there would be no conflict of interest impeding a relationship with Cedric.

Payton bit back a curse.

The fact that a man was the strongest driving force behind her desire to give up on her dream collided with every ounce of self-righteous feminism she possessed. Granted, she had never burned a bra or anything, but how would she face herself in the mirror each day if she threw away this lifelong dream she'd worked so hard for because of a man who barely spoke ten words to her a few minutes ago?

Payton's shoulders shrunk with shame, as if her fellow coffee lovers could read the thoughts going through her mind right now and were judging her for them.

She had never been one to cower and she sure as heck wasn't going to start now. She would not accept the offer for partner. She was a sports agent. She lived and worked by her own set of rules, and there was nothing Daniel McNamara or Cedric Reeves could do to change that.

# *Chapter 11*

Cedric locked up his SUV and headed for the elevators in Newark International Airport's short-term parking garage. As the elevator doors closed, he sent up a silent *thank you* that it was empty. He wasn't in the right frame of mind for dealing with fans today. Hell, he hadn't been in the right frame of mind for dealing with just about anything for the past few weeks, not since the morning he'd spent turning Payton's body inside out.

God, he could still taste her on his tongue, honey sweet and as addicting as any drug. His stomach clenched at the memory.

"Dammit," Cedric said in a fierce whisper. This entire situation was driving him out of his ever-loving mind.

He'd forced himself to forget about her. She wanted professional? That's what he'd given her. She wanted to handle everything through email? Fine. He knew how to use a computer. They didn't have to speak again if that was the way she wanted this strictly business thing to operate.

But she'd had to come out from behind the cyberspace wall she'd been hiding behind these past few weeks. She was too much of a professional to ask for a personal favor through email.

As Cedric made his way through ticketing and the security checkpoint, he went into autopilot, signing autographs and posing for camera phone pictures with the faithful Sabers fans who treated him as though he'd just made their entire year.

He spotted Payton at a snack kiosk a few steps beyond their gate. Cedric walked up to her just as the cashier was handing her a bag of cashews mixed with yogurt-covered raisins.

"Hello," Cedric said.

"Thanks for coming," Payton answered.

"Did you think I would stand you up after you bought a first-class ticket?" he said, lifting his boarding pass.

She stared at the slip of paper in his hand. "I knew you'd show," she said. Her eyes rose back to his. "You're a professional."

He was starting to hate that word. It was what had started this crap between them in the first place. He was tired of this tiptoeing dance routine they'd been engaged in these past three weeks. He wanted the Payton he'd known before Torrian and Paige's engagement party.

But as she excused herself and headed for their gate, Cedric wasn't sure that person even existed for him anymore. Was there a way to bridge the chasm that had widened between them? Or would it be easier to just get through these next few months, until they were done with his contract negotiations and Payton had fulfilled the contract they'd agreed upon when he'd signed on with Mosely Sports Management? Then he could start the agent search again.

At this point it seemed his best option. He couldn't spend the rest of his football career with an agent who barely spoke to him.

A voice called out over the loudspeaker for their plane to start boarding. Cedric encountered more fans as he made his way to the gangway with the other first-class passengers, shaking hands and accepting pats on the back for his performance so far this season.

When he noticed Payton still sitting on one of the uncomfortable chairs at the gate, Cedric went over to her.

"We're boarding," he said.

"I know," she answered. "I'm in Group Two."

"You booked me in first class, yet you're flying coach?"

She hesitated a moment. "I'm used to flying coach. I figured you weren't."

Cedric's fists clenched in frustration. Her excuse was bull and they both knew it. This was just another way for her to avoid him. But she couldn't dodge him the entire weekend. It was time they got past this. Even if he dropped her as his agent during the off-season, they still had months of working together ahead of them, and he'd be damned if he spent them swimming in this pool of awkward conversation. They were going to hash this out once and for all.

The gate agent made the last call for first-class passengers. Cedric turned toward the gangway, but not before leaving Payton with a promise.

"We're talking when this plane lands in Texas."

* * *

One would think they'd spent the entire three-hour flight from New York to Midland, Texas, in turbulence by the level of anxiety Payton had experienced from the moment the plane had gone wheels-up. But the tidal wave of apprehension crashing through her veins had nothing to do with the subtle bumps jostling the airplane. It was what would happen when they landed that had her skin tingling and her chest tightening throughout the entire flight.

She'd seen the look in Cedric's eyes when he'd issued that parting message before boarding. Idle chitchat was not what he had in mind when he'd said he wanted to talk.

Payton gripped the armrest as the plane rocked again.

She had known their impending conversation would have to happen eventually. They couldn't go on the way they had these past few weeks, not if they were to have a successful business partnership. But what if he no longer wanted to be in business with her? Sure, he'd signed a contract, but she was in contract law. She knew better than most that contracts were broken everyday. Maybe Cedric thought it was worth the cost of exercising the exit clause to get out of his deal with her.

The thought of losing her only client brought on an instant panic attack, but that was nothing compared to the panic she felt at the thought of word getting out that she'd slept with her only client. Her heart raced like a thoroughbred, pumping erratically as Payton imagined the field day sports bloggers would have with *that* kind of story. It would be open season on the few female sports agents who'd worked so hard to be taken seriously in this business.

*Calm down,* Payton reminded herself.

She was jumping to conclusions. No one would find out about that morning in her apartment. As angry as he may be with her at the moment, Payton trusted Cedric not to reveal their indiscretion to anyone.

And as for losing him as a client, she couldn't believe he would sever their professional partnership, either. She had been great for Cedric's career. As far as the press was concerned, bad-boy Cedric Reeves had done a complete one-eighty. The only stories being written up about him were to highlight his amazing work on the football field and the charity work she had encouraged. No fights with fans. No wild partying. Nothing negative whatsoever. Cedric would be a fool to drop her as his agent.

No, that's not what he wanted to talk to her about, Payton surmised. It was their *other* relationship; the one Payton had been fighting since the moment their eyes first connected in the locker room after that Sabers game at the start of the season. She'd told them both for months that they would have to squash those feelings, knowing that any romantic entanglements with Cedric would be the death of her short career as an agent.

But over the past couple of weeks, Payton had begun to question that line of thinking. A person couldn't help whom they were attracted to.

Yet when she thought of opening herself to the possibility of exploring something more with Cedric, images of the myriad of beautiful women he'd been linked to over the past few years floated across her mind. How could she be sure he would ever truly give up his playboy lifestyle and commit to a serious relationship?

"Passengers and flight attendants prepare for landing," crackled the captain's voice over the loudspeaker.

Payton nestled her head against the headrest as the aircraft made its descent. She had no idea what to do about her feelings for Cedric. The one thing she did know was that things had to change. They couldn't continue the avoidance dance they'd been engaged in these past few weeks.

She and Cedric would air everything out and decide how to move forward. They had an hour-and-a-half drive from the airport to Manchac. Nothing like being confined to a rental car to force conversation.

When Payton deplaned, Cedric was waiting for her just outside the arrival gate, his duffel bag strapped over one shoulder.

"Did you check a bag?" he asked. The chill in his voice that she'd been subjected to since calling him on Monday was mysteriously missing.

"Yes," she answered. "I'm staying a few extra days. I haven't seen my mom since the spring," she continued, as if she needed to justify traveling with more luggage than he had brought.

"That's a good idea. I'm sure your mom is happy to have you home for a while."

"Uh, yeah. She is."

Was this what he'd meant by talk? They would just ease back into normal conversation as if they had not spent the past few weeks avoiding each other the way an anorexic avoids a buffet? What would that solve? She had spent the past three hours preparing rebuttals to every accusation her brain could imagine. Payton felt almost…disappointed.

Bags were already making the loop around the

carousel when they arrived. Payton reached for hers, but Cedric put a hand to her arm, holding her back.

"This one?" he asked as he lifted the bag from the carousel.

"Yes, thanks," Payton replied.

Instead of handing her bag over to her, he pulled up the handle and looked around the airport's baggage area. "How do we get to where we're going?"

"I rented a car," she said, leading the way to the car rental company. The car she'd reserved online was already waiting when they got there. Cedric put her bags in the trunk, then went around to the driver's side.

Payton closed the keys in her fist and shook her head. "I'm driving."

"No way," he said.

"You don't even know where you are, or where you're going, for that matter."

"You'll tell me. If not, my phone has a navigation app." He leaned against the driver's side door, his arms crossed over his chest. "Call me sexist, but I don't ride in the passenger seat while a woman drives."

Payton rolled her eyes. "Fine," she relented, handing him the keys and climbing into the other side of the car.

It wasn't until they'd made it through the airport traffic and had traveled on the interstate for about ten minutes that he spoke again.

"You ready to talk?" he asked.

Payton jerked her gaze to him. "I thought we had been talking."

The look he shot her way told Payton her first instincts were dead-on. Idle chitchat was not what he'd had in mind. It had been a buffer, nothing more.

"Okay," Payton said after a deep breath. She was prepared for this. "Talk."

"I won't have another week like the three we've just had," he started. "That was Gus's way of doing things, avoiding my phone calls, shooting me an email every now and then to pacify me. I refuse to go back to that, Payton."

"I'm sorry," she said. She had been the one to dictate their communication over the past few weeks. He had tried calling the Sunday afternoon after he'd left her apartment, but Payton had let both calls go to voice mail. He'd caught on pretty quickly thereafter, sticking to emails and text messages.

Could this rift have been avoided if she'd simply picked up the phone and aired things out with him that Sunday? Payton clenched her eyes tight. Way to be a professional.

"I really am sorry, Cedric."

"No, I'm the one who's sorry," he replied. He took a deep breath. "I pushed you that morning, after Torrian's party. I knew where you stood, but I wanted you and the only thing I cared about at that moment was having you. I know it makes me a bastard, but it's the truth."

Payton's stomach clenched. She'd replayed that morning over and over in her head, remembering the way they'd made love and trying to convince herself they shouldn't do it again.

"So, where does that leave us?" she asked.

"Nothing's changed," he stated. "I still want you, Payton. I know you don't think we should be together, but I've never felt this way with anyone else. Everything is just so easy when I'm with you. So…right."

The emotions in her head waged a war with what she was feeling in her heart. "You have no idea how many times this has played back and forth in my mind," she said. "As right as it may feel, I just don't know if this is a good idea."

"I'm going to prove to you that it is," he said. "We're right for each other, Payton. Sooner or later, I'm going to make you see that."

## Chapter 12

Cedric put his fork down and excused himself from the table before he could request a third helping of peach cobbler from the ladies of Manchac High School's cafeteria. If his high school had had food like this, he would have had to take up sumo wrestling instead of football.

He shook a few hands as he made his way out of the auditorium where a banquet honoring the top performers on the school's football team was being held. Exiting through a side door, Cedric stepped into the crisp, clean air and inhaled a deep breath. He needed to clear his mind.

When they had arrived in Manchac earlier that afternoon, Payton had dropped him off at his hotel before heading to her mother's where she would be spending the weekend. It had taken a Herculean dose of restraint to stop himself from begging her to join him in his hotel suite. Thoughts of her consumed him—mind and body; to the very depths of his soul. He had to figure out a way to convince that woman that they were meant to be together.

Cedric reentered the school building and headed back for the auditorium, but he spotted movement at the end of a darkened hallway. He could recognize that form from a mile away; it haunted him in his sleep. He walked toward her as quietly as possible, though quiet was hard to accomplish on the tiled flooring of the high school's corridor.

Payton didn't turn, even though Cedric knew she had to have heard him as he approached. She stood before a huge glass-encased trophy display that spanned at least fifteen feet across. The brag shelves were located right off the school's front entrance, where everyone could see them when they entered the building.

Payton stood with her arms crossed, staring at the trophies, plaques, ribbons and pictures. Cedric's eyes zeroed in on a picture of a well-built man in a Manchac Mustangs baseball cap. He was surrounded by players, two of them hoisting a huge trophy over their heads. On the man's shoulders was a little girl of about five, a too-big baseball cap shielding her eyes and a familiar smile gracing her lips.

"He was always larger than life," Payton said with a wistful murmur.

"He affected a lot of lives," Cedric replied. He nodded toward the auditorium. "I thought the line of former players wanting to say a few words about Coach Moe would never end."

A smile touched Payton's lips. "He would be cursing up a storm over tonight—too much hoopla. He never liked it when people fussed over him. He was the most no-nonsense guy you'd ever meet." She tilted her head to the side, still staring at the trophy case. After a couple of minutes of comfortable silence, she said, "He would have liked you."

"Really?"

She nodded. "Running back was his favorite position. He said quarterbacks and wide receivers always got the praise for their fancy work in the air, but running backs were the workhorses. Without their legs on the ground, the offense doesn't stand a chance."

"Smart man. I think I would have liked your dad."

"Everybody *loved* my dad, even the players who were intimidated by that big, deep voice."

"If he could have played ball, you think he would have been a running back?"

"Nah." She shook her head. "Too much brawn. He would have been a defensive player. But he still loved your position. In fact, that's how I got my name." She glanced over at him. "Walter Payton. Greatest running back to ever play the game."

"Your dad was right. Footage of Walter Payton's days with Chicago is required viewing for every member of the Sabers running core. He's hard to emulate, though."

"You're not too bad," Payton said, her mouth tipping up at the corner in the kind of smile that made him want to kiss her.

Stepping away from the trophy case, she walked a few steps over to a colorful bulletin board with flyers about everything from a 4-H bake sale to the final pep rally of the season, which would take place tomorrow afternoon in the school gymnasium.

"Being back here reminds me of why I left to do this in the first place. To become an agent," she clarified.

"This place, this game, it was his life. My dad would be so proud of me for taking that leap."

"He is," Cedric said.

Her eyes traveled back to that picture of her father carrying her on his shoulders. "Yeah, he is."

As he studied her profile while she smiled fondly at the photograph, Cedric accepted the inevitable.

He was totally, completely, indelibly in love with her.

He couldn't pinpoint what did it. Maybe it was her love and knowledge of the game that had always meant so much to him. Or how easily she could make him laugh, sometimes just by smiling. More than likely it was a combination of all of those things that made Payton the most amazing woman he'd ever encountered. One thing he knew for certain, he loved her.

The question was, what was he going to do about it?

He had to be smart in his approach. His last attempt to take things to the next level had nearly cost him the most important thing: her.

When he recalled the hurt and sadness he'd felt over the last few weeks when they had been separated… Cedric would take a knife to the gut before he put himself through that again.

There had to be something he could do. It didn't matter how long it took, he was going to figure out a way to make Payton his.

Payton jumped to her feet as Manchac's star running back scampered down the field on a sixty-three-yard run for a touchdown, bringing the score in the school's longest-running rivalry to twenty to six.

"I bet your dad would be loving this," Cedric said over the roar of cheers.

"Oh, he would have been running down the sideline right along with the running back. Dad lived for this." She nudged Cedric's shoulder as they took their seats on the bleachers. With a grin, she said, "You may have to watch out. That running back is no joke. He may be gunning for your job in the next few years."

"Nah, I'll be long gone by the time he gets to the NFL. Shelf life for a running back isn't all that long."

Payton waited until the point-after kick was up in the air and through the goal posts before she asked, "Have you thought about what you're going to do once you're done with football? You'd probably make a good sideline analyst."

Cedric shook his head and adjusted his legs in the limited space the packed bleachers afforded. "My degree is in physical therapy. I'll get my certification and work as a therapist."

"With the Sabers?"

"No." He was quiet for so long Payton thought that was the end of it, but then he said, "There's a group home in Woodbridge, New Jersey. It's for adults with disabilities, multiple sclerosis, cerebral palsy. Stuff like that." Turning his attention back to the field, he paused for another long stretch before saying, "My brother is there."

A bolt of shock zipped through her. A brother? Payton was stunned. She'd researched Cedric thoroughly before seeking him out as a client. She'd never run across a brother.

"My twin brother," Cedric expounded, as if he'd read her thoughts. "Derek. He was born with cerebral palsy." He glanced over at her again. "He's the main reason I don't want to leave the Sabers. I'm only an hour away from Woodbridge. I drive down to see him every chance I get."

Payton remained silent. She couldn't help staring at this man she'd misjudged on so many levels before getting to know him. What a surprise he'd turned out to be.

Eventually she returned her eyes to the field, but her brain continued to ruminate over what Cedric had just revealed and, more importantly, the fact that he'd revealed it to her. His brother's existence was not common knowledge. In fact, Payton would bet it was something Cedric had worked hard to keep out of the public eye. With all the articles that had been written about him over the years, not a single reporter had discovered he had a twin brother. If they had, surely she would have uncovered it.

But she hadn't had to uncover anything. He'd told her outright. He trusted her with this part of his life.

Payton was relieved the game ended at that moment. She could blame the tears that had begun to flow down her cheeks on the heightened emotion of the team winning one for her dad on this night dedicated to his memory. But the tears were for herself and what she would miss out on with the man sitting next to her.

If circumstances were different, they could have had something special.

"Hey, why the tears?" he asked, wrapping an arm around her shoulders and hugging her to his side. "There's no crying in football. Unless you're on the losing team. Then you can cry like a baby and punch out anybody who taunts you for it."

"Don't you go around punching anybody," Payton chastised with a weak grin.

"Just kidding." He chuckled. "My agent has turned me into a new man, remember?"

The more she learned about him, the more Payton realized just how amazing a man he really was. And, for the most part, it didn't have anything to do with what she'd done over these past few months. Cedric had been misrepresented in the media, shouldering a reputation he didn't deserve. All Payton had done over the course of the time they'd worked together was bring more of these good qualities into the limelight.

"Come on." He took her wrist as he started for the closest bleacher exit aisle. "I was invited to give the kids a postgame pep talk. The locker room is always more fun after a win."

Ten minutes later, Payton found herself submerged in nostalgia, standing toward the back wall of the familiar locker room. There was fresh paint on the walls and the benches sandwiched between the rows of lockers were new, but it was the same old locker room. Coach Moe's locker room.

As she watched Cedric over the heads of the high school players still in their dirt-laden uniforms, Payton could only imagine how excited her dad would have been to have a real, live NFL player giving a pep talk to kids from little ol' Manchac High. He'd probably have the same look of awe Payton witnessed on just about every face in the locker room.

How proud would her dad have been, knowing that *she* was the one who'd made this happen for the kids.

*I did it for you, too, Daddy.* She'd never felt as close to her dad as she did at this very moment. This moment was why she'd sacrificed it all. Why she'd followed her heart.

This moment made it all worth it.

Payton held back the tears that threatened to spill over. Cedric was right, there was no crying in football. Instead, a grin so wide it hurt her cheeks spread across her face.

The entire team converged on the center of the locker room, and Cedric led them in a victory chant that ended with scores of chest bumping, fist pumping and all the other violent forms of male celebration Payton would never understand. Cedric was bombarded with slaps on the back as he made his way through the crowd of smelly players.

"What are you smiling about?" he asked as he stepped up to her.

"I bet you didn't think you'd need to hit the showers after watching a football game where you weren't even on the field," she said with a laugh.

He shrugged it off. "I like this smell. It's what I'm used to."

"I happen to like this smell, too," Payton said.

"Some women like Egyptian Musk, you like dirt."

Payton gave him a playful punch. "I guess it's what I'm used to, also. I practically lived in this locker room as a kid." Over Cedric's shoulder she spotted a bare teenaged butt. "And just like old times, that's my cue to leave. What is it with boys and their total lack of inhibitions?"

Cedric glanced over his shoulder and laughed. "Come on, you're not five years old anymore. These days you can get arrested for being in here."

They left the locker room and headed for the concession stand, where her mother and other members of the Manchac Mustang Booster Club had spent most of the game selling hot dogs and Frito Pies—corn chips topped with homemade chili. As they drove her mother home, she regaled them with anecdotes of her entire season behind the concession stand that had both Payton and Cedric laughing to the point of tears. Apparently violent confrontations were not solely for the football field. Her mom's retelling of the chili-flinging fiasco during the Manchac versus Wesley game would keep Payton laughing for ages.

Cedric ignored her mother's request to be dropped off at the end of the driveway. Parking underneath the aluminum carport adjacent to the house, he and Payton accompanied her inside to make sure all was okay.

After chastising them both for making a fuss, her mother said, "Now, if you two will excuse me, I need to wash the smell of nacho cheese from my hair." She turned to Payton. "I'll probably be in bed by the time you get back from bringing Cedric to his hotel. You still have your key, don't you?"

"Of course," Payton said. "Don't wait up for me. You've had a long night. I can see myself in."

Her mother kissed her on the cheek, then turned and did the same to Cedric. His eyes widened, but the grin on his face stretched from ear to ear.

Back in the car, Cedric settled behind the steering wheel and said, "I love your mom. She's hilarious."

"That's Mom. If I have any sense of humor at all, that's where I got it from. She and my dad were a good match. Whenever he was being too serious, all it took was one look from her to put a smile on his face. I've never seen two people who loved each other more."

"Must be hard for her since he died."

"She's strong," Payton said. "I was living in Austin at the time. I offered to move back to Manchac but she wouldn't hear of it. And when I told her I was moving to New York to become a sports agent, she couldn't have been more supportive. We both knew how much Dad would have wanted this for me."

"You're a very lucky woman, Payton. You know that?"

"I do," she affirmed with a poignant smile.

The rest of the twenty-minute drive to the hotel was made in companionable silence. Cedric pulled under the portico and motioned for the valet.

"Why are you calling the valet?" Payton asked.

"Because we can't leave the car parked here," he stated matter-of-factly.

"We're not. I'm just dropping you off," she said. He slid a glance her way and a corner of his mouth hitched up in a wicked grin. "Cedric, what are you doing?"

"Stop asking questions and follow me," he said.

"Cedric," she sighed, climbing out of the car and nodding at the valet who held the door open for her. "It's been a long night and you have to wake up at an ungodly hour to get back to the airport for your flight out."

He grabbed both of her hands and gave them a light squeeze. "Stop asking questions and follow me," he repeated.

Fighting back the rush of anticipation that started a tingling hum across her skin, Payton obediently followed him into the hotel's wide revolving doors. They moved swiftly across the luxuriant lobby, with its rich, modern furnishings, vibrant floral arrangements and flowing rock waterfall behind the reception desk.

Cedric pulled her into an elevator and slipped the plastic keycard into the slot required for access to the top three floors where the penthouse suites were housed.

"Is there a reason you can't tell me what's going on?" Payton asked.

He lolled his head to the side and gave her an exasperated look. "Don't you know how surprises work?"

"You have a surprise planned for me?" Payton exclaimed. "Why didn't you tell me?"

"Because that's how they work," he said as if he were explaining it to a four-year-old. He raised her hand to his lips and pressed a light kiss over her fingers. "Yes, I've planned a surprise for you."

The elevator chimed their arrival to the top floor and Cedric urged her to go ahead of him. They walked a few steps down the hallway to his room. He inserted the keycard, ducked his head inside, then turned to her and smiled. He pushed the door open and made a sweeping gesture. "After you."

Payton's gaze narrowed at the self-assured smile on his face. She stepped into the room and gasped.

The spacious suite was bathed in the warm glow of dozens of thick pillar candles placed throughout the living area. Scores of white and yellow roses occupied every available surface, their delicate fragrance perfuming the air.

In the center of the suite's living space were two massage tables covered by fine linen and sprinkled with a smattering of rose petals. On a nearby table a silver bucket held a champagne bottle submerged in crushed ice, along with a footed, ceramic bowl filled with plump chocolate-covered strawberries.

She turned toward Cedric who was hanging up the hotel phone next to the suite's wet bar.

"I can't believe you did this," she said as he strolled toward her.

"I haven't been the easiest person to get along with these past couple of weeks," he said. "I'm hoping this will make up for it."

Payton shook her head. "Cedric, you're not the only one at fault. I've been just as difficult. As your agent, I shouldn't—"

He put a finger to her lips, silencing the rest of her apology.

"Tonight is not about you being my agent," he said. "Tonight is about showing you how much you mean to me."

Her heart turned over at his softly spoken words.

Cedric leaned forward, resting his forehead against hers. "I'm determined to make you see how great we'll be together, Payton Mosely." He placed a gentle kiss upon her lips and said, "Now go in the bathroom and strip. The masseuses will be here any minute."

## Chapter 13

As he lay on the massage table next to Payton's, Cedric let the soothing music flowing from the suite's built-in sound system lull him into a state of semiconsciousness. His mind continued to ruminate over everything he'd learned about Payton over these past two days.

This small town was so much a part of her, so much of what made her the woman she was today. These were the people who had nurtured her love of the game. It had never been more evident than tonight as he and Payton sat in the bleachers with the other fans, cheering on the team her father had coached for so many years. Cedric doubted he'd ever seen her so happy.

Actually, he had, a bit earlier, during the pregame ceremony when they'd both stood at the center of the field and watched her mother receive a plaque in honor of Coach Moe. Tears had streamed down her face, but the streaks had only added to Payton's beauty.

Cedric had held her hand through most of the first quarter and she'd accepted it without hesitation. It had felt good to give her something she needed, even if it was just his hand.

God, he loved her.

He'd been trying to pinpoint the moment he'd fallen, but the effort was futile. There wasn't some magical point in time when he'd realized Payton was everything he could ever want in a woman. She just was. That became evident the minute he'd told her about Derek. He had not trusted even his closest teammates with knowledge of his brother, but he trusted Payton. He'd put the most important elements of his life in her hands—his career, his family, all of it. And Cedric knew she wouldn't let him down.

As the masseuses wrapped up their double massages, Cedric reached across the foot-long gap separating them and captured Payton's hand. He gave it a squeeze, which she returned. She lolled her head to the side and looked over at him. A lazy, satisfied smile drew across her lips.

"Thank you for this," she said.

"There's more to come," he replied. "There's a bottle of Perrier-Jouët just dying to be opened."

Several minutes later, they were settled on the hotel suite's buttery soft leather sofa, sipping champagne and feasting on sweet strawberries. Cedric tried to concentrate on the conversation, but having Payton only a few feet away in nothing but a bathrobe and the lace panties he'd glimpsed as she'd scooted off the massage table was probably *the* most distracting thing in the world.

Unless she was naked, of course.

"You know, I never thought I'd leave this town."

She peered at him over the rim of her champagne flute, seemingly oblivious to the sweet torture he was experiencing at the moment. "Even while practicing law in Austin, I figured I'd do that for another year or so, gain experience, then come back home and open up my own practice." She took a deep breath, then sighed. "My dad's death changed everything. After he died, starting my own law practice just didn't seem like it would be enough to fulfill me anymore. I needed to do something that brought me closer to him. Which, ironically enough, required me to move away."

"Had you talked to your dad about becoming an agent?" Cedric asked.

One corner of her mouth turned up in a wry smile. "He would have had a fit after I left my job at the law firm. But he is the one who put the idea of becoming an agent into my head. Whenever I wanted something, I would start by asking for way more than I knew he would approve so I could bargain my way down to what I wanted in the first place. He used to tell me I could negotiate my way out of a lion's den."

"I think he would approve of the path you chose," Cedric said.

"I do, too." She stared absently into her champagne. "I just needed to feel closer to him, Cedric." She looked up at him. "And I do. I can feel him with me when I'm trying to close a deal, cheering me on."

"The same way you cheered on his team for so many years."

A broad smile spread across her face. "Our roles have reversed."

She reached over and plucked another strawberry from the ceramic bowl. Cedric was hit with a tidal wave of raw lust as her sensuous lips closed around the plump fruit. He was dying to crawl over to her and turn her body inside out, but he didn't want to move too fast. The fact that he'd convinced her to stay and enjoy the surprise he'd arranged was a small victory. He wouldn't push his luck.

"I have to admit, I've enjoyed this little town of yours," he said, settling on a safer subject, something that wasn't likely to stoke the fire burning in his gut. "For someone like me who's spent his entire life in the big city, this has been a bit of a culture shock. I like it, though. I like how everyone knows each other."

"That's because you didn't have to grow up here," she said around a mouth full of strawberry, amusement lighting her eyes. "And I had it worse than most, being Coach Moe's daughter. I couldn't go anywhere without being recognized, and believe me, in a town this small, anything I did would have made its way back to my folks." She laughed. "There was no need to sneak around, though. Like I said, if I wanted to do something, I negotiated my way into it."

"So I have an agent who's been cultivating her skills since high school, huh? Pretty sweet."

"I know how to drive a hard bargain when necessary."

"You don't have to tell me," he snorted. "As many times as you've shut me down, I know all too well how hard it is to bargain with you."

Cedric wanted to kick himself as soon as the words left his mouth. They were having their first totally tension-free conversation in weeks and he had to muck it up by introducing the one subject that was sure to put an end to the relaxed mood.

But true to her nature of surprising him, Payton didn't bite his head off. Instead she gazed over at him, and with a look that nearly brought him to his knees, she said, "Why don't you ask me again?"

For a moment Cedric just stared, wondering if the sultriness in her voice had been a trick of his own mind. But then she reached over and plucked the flute from his hand, placing it, along with hers, on the glass-topped coffee table.

"Ask me again, Cedric," she encouraged with a low murmur that shot a rod of electricity straight to his groin.

Cedric peered into her eyes, looking for any sign that would indicate she wasn't operating on all six cylinders, but all he found was raw honesty. And desire. A whole lot of desire.

"Since you seem to have misplaced your voice, I guess I'll have to do the asking," Payton said. "Kiss me. Please?"

"Payton—"

She halted his words, placing one deliciously soft finger against his lips.

"Don't," she murmured. "Don't say anything but yes."

At that moment he couldn't utter a syllable through the lump of desire clogging his throat. Instead, he let his actions speak for him.

Cedric pushed his hands through her hair and pulled her face to his, capturing her lips in a hot, deep, spine-tingling kiss that he felt on every inch of his skin. Payton returned the kiss with an ardor that increased his passion tenfold, pushing her tongue into his mouth as she held on to his shoulders.

It was heaven. Pure heaven.

Her hands traveled down his arms, entwining with his fingers. Cedric held on to her like a lifeline, feeding off the connection between them. It was stronger, hotter and more intense than anything he'd ever experienced.

Her mouth still mingling with his, Payton tugged him from the couch and led the way to his room.

Cedric knew once they crossed that threshold there would be no turning back.

With every drop of strength left in his bones, he pulled his mouth from hers and asked, "Payton, are you sure about this? You know what happened the last time. I don't want to see regret in your eyes in the morning."

She took a step back and stared at him with shell-shocked eyes, apparently as bowled over by the force of their kiss as he had been. Then she looked away, unable to meet his eyes. It felt as if someone had stuck a fist in his chest and squeezed his heart muscles until there was nothing left.

Payton dropped his hands and opened the door to the suite's master bedroom. She stepped into the darkened room, turned back to him and held out her hand.

The welcoming gesture caused his heart rate to skyrocket. The need apparent on her face put an end to any doubt he'd had about what she wanted. It was all too clear what she wanted.

Him.

Cedric put his hand into her warm palm and allowed her to pull him into the room.

Payton's heart pounded with a ferocity she had never before experienced as she led Cedric to the bed. She hadn't planned on this happening tonight. She had planned to bid him farewell when she dropped him off at the hotel's front entrance, and not see him again until they were both back in New York. But now that they were here, she couldn't imagine another place she'd rather be than with this man who'd managed to charge past all the reasons she'd formed to keep them apart.

She backed up until the backs of her legs hit the bed, then she sat on the edge, pulling Cedric to stand between her spread knees. She loosened the belt at his waist, opening the robe, her fingertips tingling as she grazed them across his tight abs. The corded muscles felt like silk-covered ropes.

Cedric groaned, dipping his head down and seizing her lips in a kiss Payton felt all the way to her toes. She moved from his lips to the muscled torso she'd been fantasizing about since the morning they'd first made love, peppering his silky, chocolate skin with delicate kisses. Cedric wrapped both hands behind her head, another low groan escaping his lips.

She cupped him through his boxers, wrapping a fist around his erection, but he quickly pulled her hand away.

"I'm hanging on by a thread, baby. I'd never last if you do that."

He sought her mouth again, his tongue darting in and out as he gently lowered her to the bed and covered her body with his own. Payton skimmed her hands up his sides, pushing the robe off his shoulders. She clutched his solid back, holding him in place as he deepened their kiss.

He was like air. Essential. Life-giving. Everything she needed.

As Cedric undid the tie at the front of her robe, the pulse thrumming between her thighs escalated to the point of pain. She needed him like she needed her next breath.

"Oh, God. Cedric, please," Payton pleaded.

He found her neck, nibbling and biting from the curve

of her jaw down to her collarbone. His head dipped lower and he sucked her distended nipple into his mouth. Payton pushed him away just long enough to pull her robe completely off. Skin-to-skin contact wasn't just needed, it was necessary. She had to feel him against her.

As he covered her body, she closed her eyes and floated into her own version of heaven on earth.

The silky softness of Payton's delectable skin set his body on fire. Her nipple grazed his chest and his body grew even harder.

Damn, she felt good.

Cedric trailed his tongue down the valley between her breasts, teasing the skin with his teeth. As he licked the underside of her breast his hand inched lower, finding the black lace panties he would dream about for years to come. He slipped his hand inside the delicate fabric and zeroed in on her moist center. It pulsed against his fingers, hot, slick, slippery.

He was dying to taste her.

Cedric worked his way down her belly, punctuating the flat plane with hungry kisses. He pulled the panties down her hips and legs, kissing her inner thigh, behind her knee, the sole of her foot. Then he moved back up, his mind focused on that one spot he craved more than anything.

He squeezed the softness of her thighs as he pushed them apart, working his way to her center with deliberate slowness, taking his time as he worshiped her body. Payton let out a soft moan that traveled like fingers down his spine. She gripped his shoulders, then brought her hands around his head, pulling him toward that spot.

Cedric stopped just short of giving her what he knew she needed.

He wanted her to ask for it.

He tilted his head to the side and drew light circles along her inner thigh, taking a gentle love bite before turning his attention to the other thigh.

"Cedric, please," Payton moaned.

That's all it took. He settled his head between her legs and lost himself in her flavor. He stroked his tongue up and down her hot, wet center, flicking it over and around the bundle of tight nerves at her cleft. He pulled the nub between his lips and sucked hard, feeding off her soft cries of pleasure.

Payton captured his head in her hands and held him there as her body rose to meet his mouth. Cedric met her demands, drilling inside of her with his tongue, learning every part of her most intimate place, loving her taste and texture.

His finished with one final sweep of his tongue up her delicate slit. Then he rose and stared down at the vision that lay before him. She was glorious, her body flush and glistening. Cedric was so hard he couldn't think past the thought of joining his body with hers.

He pushed up from the bed.

Payton grabbed his hand. "Where are you going?" she panted.

"Don't worry, love. I'm not about to leave you."

He walked over to his carryall bag and grabbed the pack of condoms he'd packed with a slim hope that he would have a use for them. He ripped the package open and rolled the latex over his straining erection as he walked back to the bed. His arms trembling, Cedric fitted himself between Payton's legs and sank into the most amazing heat he'd ever felt. She was hot, silky and so tight he could hardly stand it. She closed around his pulsing erection as if she was made exclusively for him. He moved in and out of her, up and down, her body cloaking him.

Payton's back bowed off the bed as she spread her legs even farther, reached down and grabbed his butt. Cedric hissed as her fingernails sank into his flesh. The mixture of pleasure and pain was so erotic. He gripped her hips and pounded into her, over and over and over, plunging into her hot, moist flesh. With one final thrust he came with a blinding rush of white light and pure pleasure.

His body suddenly weak, he fell onto Payton, his cheek finding a soft place upon her breast.

Cedric wasn't sure how much time had passed before he lifted his head. He'd thought she was sleeping by the even movement of her chest, but when he looked up he found Payton staring back at him, a glow of satisfaction surrounding her.

Cedric scooted a few inches up, needing to touch her at all times. He rested his head on a pillow, facing her. The moonlight coming through the sheer curtain cut an ethereal swath across her face, making it even more beautiful, if that were possible. For untold minutes, they lay face-to-face. Words were unnecessary. Cedric saw everything he needed to know staring back at him in her liquid brown eyes.

After some time, Payton captured one of his hands and brought it to her lips, brushing a featherlight kiss across his knuckles.

"Tell me about your brother," she said. "Please?"

Cedric's first instinct was to change the subject, but as he stared into her eyes, the concern and understanding staring back at him was enough to lift the shield on this part of his life he kept hidden from so many.

"Derek was born just two and a half minutes after I was, but we're as different as night and day. He was born with cerebral palsy." Cedric shut his eyes tight and shook his head. "I ask God all the time why him and not me."

"That kind of questioning will drive you crazy," Payton said. "It's like me asking why my dad had to die so young. Who knows why these things happen?"

"Well, I know why it happened to Derek," Cedric said. He looked away, not wanting to see the dismay on her face when he spoke his next words. "It was my fault," he revealed. "Doctors said while we were in the womb I consumed most of the nutrients, not leaving enough for Derek to fully develop."

"It's not as if you did that on purpose."

Cedric's eyes snapped up at the incredulousness in her voice. None of the disgust he thought he'd see was there. "If it were not for me, my brother would be healthy. Normal. Because of me, he's going to be in a wheelchair his entire life."

Payton squeezed his hand and brought it back to her lips. "Cedric, please tell me you haven't blamed yourself for this your entire life? You have to know this isn't your fault. It's nature."

"Doctors tried to tell me that over the years, but how can I not feel guilty, Payton? Here I am, healthy, strong, living my dream, and all because I stole what should have belonged to my brother."

"You can't blame yourself for your brother's condition. Think of all the children who are born with cerebral palsy who are not twins. The same could have happened to Derek." She kissed his forearm and hugged him closer to her. "It wasn't your fault, Cedric."

He'd researched the disease for years and knew there were a number of different things that could have caused his brother to be born the way he was. He'd shouldered the guilt for so long, Cedric had not allowed himself to consider that he wasn't the cause of Derek's condition.

Cedric shook his head. "He looks up to me as if I'm some kind of hero. Nothing makes him happier than telling people about his big brother, the NFL star."

"Sounds as if he's an even bigger football fan than I am."

"I'm not sure anyone is as big a fan as you are." Cedric chuckled, then he sobered, the moment of lightheartedness replaced with grim determination. "I'm done jeopardizing my career." He grasped her hands and held on tight, needing her to understand the depths of his resolve. "Everything I do on that field, I do it for Derek. I now realize that what I do *off* the field can have just as big of an effect on him. I can't risk losing my career. It's all Derek has."

"Your career isn't all your brother has," Payton whispered, her eyes covered with a sheen of tears. "He has you. But if it's your career with the Sabers you're worried about, then don't. This is my personal guarantee, you're going to be with the team for many years to come."

She wrapped her arms around his neck and pulled him in for a kiss. Before he could utter the words *I love you,* Payton covered his mouth with her own, thrusting her tongue inside. Even though he didn't say the words, he felt them in every fiber of his being. And as he slowly made love to her again, Cedric was determined to show her with his body the words he didn't have a chance to say with his mouth.

## Chapter 14

Payton sat with one leg folded underneath her while she used the other to push the rocking chair into a gentle sway. She wrapped the crocheted afghan more securely around her shoulders as she stared at nothing across the lawn. Her mind was a thousand miles away—or however many miles it was to Baltimore, where the Sabers were playing today. But her mind wasn't on the team, just their star running back.

What was she going to do?

She'd defied her number one rule. She'd fallen in love with her client.

There was no denying her feelings for Cedric, not after the love they'd shared while wrapped in each other's arms. Now she had to decide what to do about those feelings.

Payton knew she didn't really have a choice. What happened three weeks ago could be labeled a mistake—a slip in judgment. But she'd known exactly what she was doing last night. And if she had her way, she would continue doing it every night for the rest of her life. How could she and Cedric ever go back to the way things were?

It was simple. They *wouldn't* go back. She needed Cedric in her life, and not just as her client. Somehow, they would have to figure out a way to make this work.

"What are you doing out here? The game's about to start."

Payton tracked her mother's steps as she made her way across the porch. She came bearing gifts, a tray with hot tea and a plate of the shortbread cookies she'd baked earlier that day. Her mother sat the tray on the small table dividing the two rockers.

"You mind?" her mother asked, perched just above the other rocker.

"Please. Sit." Payton gestured. She took one of the mugs and sipped her tea, a small smile lifting her lips at the familiar taste of honey and cinnamon.

"I should ask what you're doing out here when there's football on, but I think I know," her mother said, staring out over the lawn. She lifted a cookie from the tray and took a bite. "He's a nice young man."

"'Young' being the operative word there."

"He's not that much younger than you are," her mother chastised.

"I know," Payton said, exasperated. The couple of years age difference hadn't worked as a good excuse when she'd tried it on herself. "It has nothing to do with his age. But he *is* my client."

"And?"

She looked over at her mother. "And? How would it look if I fell in love with my client?"

"First, I don't think there's any *if* about it. I can tell by the way you look at him that you're already in love with him, or pretty close to it."

She shut her eyes in an attempt to block out the truth of her mother's words.

"And, second," her mom continued, "why does it matter what people think?"

"It just does." Payton shoved her fingers through her hair. "I've spent all this time trying to present myself as a professional who is no different from any other sports agent. The worst thing I could do is fall in love with my very first client. Talk about girlie."

Her mother reached over and covered Payton's hand. "I can list about a thousand other things you could do that would be worse than falling in love with Cedric Reeves." Her mother sat back and took a sip of her tea. "I've told you how your grandfather felt about your father when he started to court me, haven't I?"

Payton's lips lifted in a smile as she remembered the story. "You said Granddad wouldn't let him in the house."

"The house? He wouldn't let him on the porch steps. He didn't want his baby girl dating one of those Mosely boys from the east side of Manchac."

"As if the west side of Manchac is all that different," Payton snorted.

"It was back then, but it didn't matter to me. I fell in love with one of those Mosely boys and I didn't care what anyone else thought about it. You can't let other people decide who you're going to love, Payton."

"But what if people no longer take me seriously as an agent?"

"You make them," her mother said. "They didn't take you seriously before Cedric became your client, but you made them stand up and take notice. No one said this agent business was going to be easy. You knew it was going to be a fight from the very beginning. But you're doing it, and you're going to keep doing it.

"But you also have to do what makes you happy." Her mother squeezed her hand. "And Cedric makes you happy. Every time I saw the way he looked at you I wanted to give him a hug, or a kiss, or another slice of pie, or something."

Payton laughed at that. "I think Cedric got out of here just in time. He probably gained five pounds over these last two days."

"I'm sure he'll burn it off during the course of that game today. Which we are missing sitting out here on this porch." Her mother tugged her hand. "Come on. You and your father made me watch games every Sunday during football season. No use breaking the tradition."

When her mother went to extract her hand, Payton held on to it.

"Thank you," she said.

Her mother nodded, giving her hand another firm squeeze before letting go.

They spent the afternoon watching the Sabers beat up on Baltimore. With that win, which was capped off by Cedric's twenty-yard highlight reel-worthy run into the end zone, the Sabers earned themselves a spot in the playoffs. And Cedric's standout performance would give Payton more ammunition when it was time to renegotiate his contract in a few weeks.

The next morning, Payton awoke to the smell of coffee mingling with her mother's homemade cinnamon rolls. Her stomach rumbled in anticipation. She joined her mother in the kitchen and headed straight for the coffee and pastries.

"Don't touch that," her mother said. "I just drizzled the icing on them. They still need to cool."

Payton waited until her mother left the room before she ignored the warning and scooped up a gooey cinnamon roll. The first bite seared the tip of her tongue.

"I told you not to touch them," came the call from the living room.

Payton rolled her eyes as she grabbed an ice cube from the freezer. She would eventually learn to listen to that woman.

"Payton, come here. You need to see this."

The urgency in her mother's voice caused Payton's heart to pump faster.

When she reached the living room, her mother pointed to the television where an ESPN anchor sat behind a news desk. The shot changed to a shaking, low-quality video—like something shot with a cell phone. At least five people jockeyed and wrestled, a medley of elbows and fists colliding with chests and jaws. In the midst of the melee, Payton recognized Cedric. The picture blurred as it zoomed in to his face, then cleared just as another man shoved a hand under his chin.

"No, he did *not* get into a fight," Payton said through clenched teeth.

She ran to her bedroom and grabbed her cell phone from her purse. There was a text message from him that came at eleven-fifteen last night.

*I need u. In B-more. Plz come.*

Payton punched his number into her phone, but it went straight to voice mail. She stuffed her clothes into her travel bag with one hand and dialed the airline with another. She had to leave in ten minutes if she wanted any chance of making the next flight out of Midland to Baltimore.

Her mother came to stand in the doorway. "Is there anything I can do?"

"Try to convince me not to kill him when I see him," Payton said.

"Killing him would be a bad thing," her mother said in a calm voice.

Payton crammed her cosmetics clutch into the bag. "He's been on thin ice all season long. And now at the very end of the season, just when everything is going great, he gets into a barroom brawl."

Payton could actually feel the blood boiling in her veins. Everything they'd worked for was shot to hell. How was she going to convince Sabers upper management that Cedric had changed? She wasn't all that convinced herself.

A half hour into the eighty-mile drive to the airport, Payton received a text message from Cedric. He was on his way back to New York. The Sabers were planning a two o'clock press conference to address last night's incident.

It took the rest of the drive to Midland International Airport and the entire flight back to New York for Payton to calm herself down. When she pulled into the parking lot at the Sabers practice facility, Payton sat behind the wheel of her car for several long moments, going over the plan she'd devised while on the flight. She only hoped her spin on whatever had happened last night would fly with reporters.

The building was busier than she'd anticipated. The team was usually off on Mondays, but with just one more game before the start of the playoffs, it looked as if players and coaches were trying to gain an edge with extra preparation. Payton was led down a hallway that was an offshoot of the wide corridor that led to the locker room.

Seated around an oval table in the meeting room were Cedric and two of his teammates, Jared Dawson and Randall Robinson, along with the Sabers head coach, Dave Foster, the team's general manager and another man in a suit Payton had never seen before.

Cedric pushed from the table and rushed over to her. "Thanks for coming," he said.

"What were you thinking?" Payton seethed.

His eyebrows shot up. "You think last night was my fault?"

"It's hard to deny video evidence," she retorted.

Cedric grabbed her arm and pulled her into the hallway, closing the door behind them. Payton jerked away from him and railed, "How could you be so irresponsible? You know what happened last year in Baltimore, yet you deliberately put yourself in a position to land in trouble. And even worse, you get caught on video!"

"So that's it? I'm the bad guy here?"

Payton pointed a finger at the conference room. "It's splattered all over the television!"

Cedric crossed his arms over his chest and pierced her with a searing glare. "And just what did you see on the video, Payton?"

"I saw..." Payton tried to remember exactly what she saw. It was mostly a lot of fist flailing and general hoopla.

"I'll tell you what you saw," Cedric said, taking two giant steps forward until he'd backed her up against the wall. His face stopped mere inches from hers. "You saw two drunken Baltimore fans gang up on me, but you didn't see me throw a single punch. Not even to defend myself." He stepped even closer. "Maybe you should get the entire story before you hand down a guilty verdict.

"There are a couple of other videos that have popped up since last night. They show Jared and Randall pulling those guys off of me and the three of us leaving the club."

Payton was at a loss for words.

"I didn't start this fight," Cedric continued. "I didn't finish it, either. I walked away." The look he trained on her cut Payton to the quick. "Even Coach took the time to hear my side of the story before automatically assuming this was my fault. At least he had faith in me, but I guess it's asking too much of you to believe I've changed over these past few months."

His frustration was palpable, but Payton refused to bear the brunt of it. She was not the guilty party here.

"I wake up this morning to your name splattered all over the television and video evidence of you in a fight! What was I supposed to think?"

"That you could trust me not to go back on my word," he suggested in an accusing voice. "I promised you I wouldn't do anything to jeopardize my chances of re-signing with the team. Is it too much to expect that you could believe in me? I thought we'd gotten to that point, Payton, in both our professional and personal relationships." He took another step back. "But I guess I was wrong."

Payton stared at his face, remembering the expression it held just two nights ago while they'd lain wrapped in each other's arms. They'd both opened their souls to each other, sharing their pasts and their hopes for the future. Cedric was a different man. He'd acknowledged that. Why hadn't she?

He had a right to be upset. From the moment she saw the video, she hadn't even allowed herself to consider that Cedric had not been at the center of the incident. His earlier promises had meant nothing to her.

"Cedric." Payton closed her eyes and took a deep breath. "I'm sorry," she said. What else could she say at this point? He was angry and had every right to be.

"It's all good." He backed away and shrugged. "At least I know where we stand."

"Cedric," Payton called again. She reached for him but he pulled away.

"No. Forget it." The set of his jaw was hard as stone. "It's nothing I haven't been through before. I'm getting used to the way you agents operate."

His cold words lanced her chest, cutting to the very core of her being.

Payton followed him into the conference room and joined the others at the table. She was introduced to Mark Paxton from the Sabers public relations department. He attached a laptop to an overhead projector.

"So far, two additional videos have popped up on YouTube. The one I'm about to pull up shows the fight from start to finish. It's almost as if whoever was filming it knew something was about to go down."

Payton settled into her seat, which was directly across the table from Cedric, as the additional footage from last night's incident rolled on the screen.

Jealousy gripped Payton's chest as several ladies— though Payton felt generous in calling them such— approached Cedric's table, their objective obvious as they sidled their scantily clad bodies up to the stars in the club. One of the women bent low and whispered something in Cedric's ear.

Payton studied the screen with an intensity that shocked her, so intent was she to see Cedric's response to the blatant come-on. He smiled at the woman but shook his head in the negative.

Payton slowly let out the breath she'd been holding. She looked across the table to find Cedric staring at her. The grim set to his jaw told her he knew exactly what she thought his reaction was going to be to the flirting women. Disappointment was evident in his eyes, but there was something else there.

Anger.

In that moment Payton realized she'd just added insult to injury. Not trusting him to stay out of trouble was one thing. Believing he would cheat on her showed a complete lack of trust—one he didn't deserve.

"This is the part we need to show at the press conference," Mark Paxton said.

Payton brought her eyes back to the screen.

Two men approached Cedric's table. There were clearly some harsh words tossed back and forth, then one of the men took a swing at Cedric. He ducked, but instead of countering with a defensive swing—something Payton would have done herself at that point—he held his hands up, visibly trying to calm the situation. It was the second guy who came from the other side of the screen and grabbed Cedric in a choke hold who lit the fire on the powder keg.

Pandemonium ensued, with Jared and Randall trying to pull the guy off of Cedric. Cedric wrenched free of the choke hold and grabbed Jared from the fray.

"So, exactly what happened?" Tom Rutledge, the team's general manager, asked.

"It's just what you saw," Cedric replied. "We were sitting there minding our own business. Women had been coming up to the table all night—it's what happens when we're out—" he looked pointedly at Payton "—whether we ask for it or not. A couple of the local guys didn't like that, so they came to the table to tell us."

"Ced already has a bad reputation in Baltimore," Jared added. "You know, from that thing with the fan last year."

"That was *last* year," Cedric stated. "I've done everything by the book this year. Been the model player both on and off the field. The media hyped this up and automatically labeled me as the bad guy. They didn't even bother to get the entire story first, they just assumed Cedric Reeves was back to his old ways." He zeroed his gaze in on Payton again. "I guess what they say is true," Cedric huffed ironically. "Once a troublemaker, always a troublemaker."

Payton started to speak but Tom Rutledge beat her to it.

"It's evident that you had nothing to do with this, Cedric. We'd originally called the press conference to tell the press we were looking into the matter and would comment later, but with this other video that has popped up there's no need to wait for later. We're going to go out there, tell the people we're behind you and that'll be the end of it."

"The big boys at the network will be happy about this," Mark Paxton said. "This is the kind of press they like. Scandal equals ratings, but this time more people will tune in to the game because they'll feel bad that they jumped to the wrong conclusion about you."

Cedric's eyes flashed to hers. "Seems to be happening a lot."

The accusation in his voice quadrupled Payton's guilt.

"Let's go meet the press," Coach Foster said. "The sooner we put this behind us, the better. We don't need any distractions going into the playoffs."

One by one they filed out of the conference room. Payton held back, needing to clear the air with Cedric before they stood in front of those cameras.

"Cedric," she called before he could leave the room.

Jared Dawson stood just inside the door. He looked from Cedric to Payton, then back to Cedric, who motioned for his teammate to leave. Cedric turned to her and crossed his arms over his chest. To say the look on his face was ominous was a gross understatement.

"I was wrong," Payton admitted.

"Yes, you were," he agreed. "But it doesn't matter."

"Yes, it does," she said.

"To you, maybe. For me, this is just par for the course. Now, if you'll excuse me, I need to go and clear my name."

Payton almost called after him again but stopped herself. She knew she would only get more derision, which was exactly what she deserved.

Cedric stood just to the left of the Sabers head of public relations as the guy told the crowd of reporters that the Sabers organization was behind Cedric one hundred percent regarding the incident in Baltimore last night. But after his opening statement, Cedric tuned out Mark Paxton's words. His mind was too busy rehashing his earlier exchange with Payton.

Cedric had never experienced a knife to the gut, but he doubted it could hurt worse than the stab of pain he'd felt when she'd walked into the conference room and looked at him with eyes full of accusation.

He'd done a few boneheaded things when he first entered the NFL, but that was nearly four years ago. He'd mellowed out since then and had completely overhauled his image these past few months. Payton had been right there with him. She'd been an integral part of his transformation. Yet after all the time they'd shared, after the night he'd held her in his arms and pledged that he was never turning back to his old ways, all it took was a ten-second video on YouTube to convince her otherwise. His words meant nothing.

Cedric continued to stare straight ahead, his eyes glossing over the crush of reporters who had come expecting to hear that the Sabers had finally kicked their troubled star running back to the curb. At least his team had an ounce of faith in him. It was more than he could say for the woman standing next to him. The woman he'd entrusted with his career.

With his heart.

Despite the announcement from Mark Paxton that there would be no questions taken after the statement, the reporters still shouted a bevy of inquiries at the people on the podium. Coach Foster declined to answer any of them, thanked the reporters for coming and led the march out of the press room.

Cedric stayed back to chat with the coach, hoping Payton would take the hint and leave. But she lingered in the wide corridor that led from the press room to the locker room. After ten minutes, Cedric realized she wasn't going anywhere. He left the coach and strolled to where Payton stood.

"Can we talk about this, please?" she asked.

Cedric crossed his arms over his chest and shrugged. "What's there to talk about?"

She clenched her eyes tight and let out a frustrated sigh. "I can see that you're angry, and I'm fine with that. You have every right to be."

"I'm not angry," Cedric interjected. "*Enlightened* would be a better word. I have a clearer picture of exactly what you think of me."

"Cedric, that isn't fair. All I had to go on was that video."

"Exactly," he accused, stepping forward and getting right in her face. "You didn't even give me the benefit of the doubt. You just automatically assumed I was in the wrong."

Cedric tried to tamp down his hurt and anger but it was no use. He saw every dream he'd had for them crumbling before his eyes, and it hurt even more than her lack of faith. Pain lanced through him at the thought of losing her, but after what he saw today she was already lost to him.

"You want to know what isn't fair, Payton? You making me think you believed in me."

She held her hands out, pleading. "I do believe in you, Cedric. It was wrong for me to jump to conclusions. I know that and I'm sorry. But—"

"But what? What else is there to say?" He pointed a finger at her. "You know, I should have expected this. Gus Houseman did the same thing. When the going got rough, he bailed."

"I am not bailing on you."

"No," Cedric stated. "I'm the one who's bailing on you. My agent is supposed to be my strongest supporter. You can't support me if you don't have faith that I'll keep my word."

Cedric didn't give her a chance to respond. Turning on his heels, he called on every bit of strength within his bones as he walked down the hallway and out of the Sabers facility.

Even before she'd paid a ridiculous amount of money to park in the garage next to Cedric's building, Payton's gut had told her this trip would be pointless. She wasn't on the visitor's list, so the building's concierge wouldn't allow her past the front entrance without first calling Cedric.

Payton had known by the frown that had pulled at the man's mouth what Cedric's reply had been when the concierge had asked if it was okay to allow Payton up to his condo. With an indulgent smile he'd apologized and suggested that if she wanted Cedric's autograph, she should try to catch him at Sabers Stadium after a home game where most players met fans.

She hadn't bothered to inform him that she was Cedric's agent, not just some random fan. Honestly, she didn't know if the statement was true anymore. If the way things had ended between them after the press conference was any indication, more than likely she was not going to be Cedric's agent for much longer.

The thought of being alone chafed like sandpaper on her skin, so instead of going home, Payton had dipped into the sports bar a few blocks from her apartment building. Two hours later, she was still here, nursing her fourth cherry cola.

She looked up at the flat screen above the bar. Theo Stokes shared a news desk with two other former football pros-turned-sports commentators. The TV was muted, but Payton didn't need the sound to know what was being said as a clip of today's press conference appeared on the screen. The episode played over and over in her head like a highlight reel.

She had no one to blame but herself. Cedric was right; she hadn't given him the benefit of the doubt. From the moment she'd seen the clip of the bar fight, she'd judged, tried and convicted him in her mind. It had not even occurred to her that someone else could be at fault.

How could she claim to be a credible agent when she automatically believed the worst about her own client? She should have walked into that conference room and convinced Sabers management of Cedric's innocence, not the other way around. It took more than just knowledge of the game to be a good agent. It took a faith and commitment to her client that she hadn't exhibited today.

Maybe she wasn't cut out for this business after all.

The thought had rolled around in her head all too often over the past couple of hours, and her actions today proved her point. She'd given up on Cedric, losing his respect.

But she'd lost so much more than just her client's respect today. She'd lost the man she loved.

Above the clank of glassware hitting the bar and the chatter of about two dozen bar patrons, Payton heard the chime of her cell phone. She dove for her purse, frantically searching for her phone, hoping to see Cedric's number.

But when she retrieved the phone, it wasn't Cedric's name that illuminated the tiny screen.

As she stared at the phone through another trilling chime, Payton tried to swallow the lump of disappointment that welled in her throat. Regret over her colossal failure as an agent collided with disappointment in what she was about to do. But at this point, Payton saw no other choice.

She answered the phone.

"Hello, Daniel. I assume you're calling to tell me the position at McNamara and Associates is still available."

## Chapter 15

As he watched the clock on the Sabers giant scoreboard tick down to zero, Cedric could not summon the desire to care that after a stellar season, the Sabers had just been knocked out of the playoffs by a sixteen-point underdog. He'd given the game everything he'd had, shattering the team's all-time rushing record in a single game. But his heart hadn't been in it. His heart hadn't been in anything for the past two weeks. Not since he'd left Payton at the Sabers facility after the press conference.

Cedric followed his teammates off the field, not even bothering to look up as the loyal Sabers fans shouted his name. He was in automatic mode as he stripped out of his uniform and entered the shower, counting the tiles in the shower stall in an attempt to keep his mind clear of the erotic images he tortured himself with in his showers at home. That would be a hard one to explain to his teammates—pun intended.

Cedric made quick work of dressing, wanting to get through the postgame interviews as soon as possible so he could head home. Though God only knew why he was in such a rush. After losing today's season-ending game, he suddenly had a lot of time on his hands.

As Cedric made his way to his locker, he spotted agent extraordinaire Marvin Hayes standing right in front of his cubby. Hayes was *the* agent. His client list covered every sport imaginable and he only represented the cream of the crop, including two former Super Bowl MVPs, last year's Cy Young award winner in baseball and the current heavyweight boxing champ of the world.

For Cedric it was like déjà vu. He couldn't help but recall the last time a sports agent met him at his locker after a game. Had that only been a few months ago? In some ways it seemed as if he'd known Payton forever; yet these days she felt like a stranger.

That deep ache that had become a part of his existence whenever he even thought her name settled into his bones. He would have to embrace the misery. There was no getting over this.

As Cedric approached, Marvin Hayes extended his hand. "Good game out there today," he said. "Two hundred eighty-eight rushing yards in a single game? That's phenomenal."

Cedric gripped the proffered palm. "Doesn't mean much when you lose."

"Just wait until the sting of the loss wears off. It'll mean a lot when we renegotiate your contract in a few weeks."

"We?" Cedric asked.

A cagey smile pulled at Hayes's lips. "I don't like to play games with my clients, Cedric."

"I'm not a client," he returned.

"Not yet. But you're smart and you know what it would mean if you walked into the meeting with Sabers upper management with me by your side."

He *did* know. The deals Marvin Hayes had negotiated for his star clients were legendary. The man commanded respect. And he hardly ever took on new clients. Cedric hadn't even bothered to call him during his frantic agent search. Yet here was Hayes, already claiming Cedric as his new client.

And where was his current agent? Nowhere to be found. She hadn't even bothered to show up at today's game.

Hayes clamped a hand on Cedric's back. "Why don't we talk after your postgame interviews? I think you'll like what I have to offer."

Payton folded her legs underneath her and wrapped her purple and black Manchac Mustangs afghan more securely around her arms. Watching the snow fall on Buffalo Stadium made her shiver, even though she was in the comfy warmth of her living room.

As the seconds ticked down to halftime of the game between New England and Buffalo, she picked up the file folder from her coffee table so she could do a little work before the start of the third quarter. She needed to do another read-through of the contract she'd drawn up for Percy Johnson. Now that the Sabers season had come to an end in today's earlier divisional playoff game, the young player would have an earlier start to his off-season.

The bookies in Las Vegas were no doubt having a field day with all the money they were raking in. This was supposed to be the year the Sabers made it to the

Super Bowl. No one had expected them to get knocked out so early. It was the nature of the playoffs. A missed tackle here, a couple of costly turnovers there and your season was over.

Payton tried to shake off her disappointment. As an agent, she could not let her emotions about the game get the best of her. When her agency started growing, she would likely have clients who played on opposing teams. She could not allow her heart to get entrenched in a single team's season.

Payton turned her attention back to Percy's contract. Convincing the rookie linebacker that he should sign with Mosely Sports Management hadn't been as hard as Payton had once thought it would be. She'd had calls from several Sabers players, a tight end for the Giants, even a power forward with the New Jersey Nets, though she had no desire to move into the NBA arena. After all, she became an agent to stay close to the game of football.

The flood of calls had started Tuesday, the same day she'd turned down Daniel McNamara's offer to return to the firm for the very last time. Tuesday had also been the day it was announced that Cedric Reeves would be the face of Electronic Sports Gaming's newest football video game. News of the eight-figure endorsement deal Payton had scored for her client had buzzed through the NFL's grapevine at rapid speed, and had several players rethinking the girl agent.

Too bad she couldn't enjoy a single bit of her success.

She and Cedric hadn't spoken a word to each other since the press conference. He hadn't answered his phone when she'd called to give him the news about the ES Gaming deal and Payton hadn't bothered to call back. They'd done the communication-through-nonverbal-devices-only dance before; in fact, the steps were still fresh in her mind.

They would have to speak face-to-face eventually. The NFL's free-agency period would open up in a matter of weeks and she and Cedric still had to go over the list of incentive clauses and performance bonuses they would demand during contract negotiations. After the stellar season he'd had, Payton had much more ammunition than when she'd first taken him on as a client a few months ago.

What happened after their meeting with the Sabers was still up in the air. Now was not the time to worry about that. Everything she and Cedric had accomplished this entire season would mean nothing if he walked out of that meeting without a new contract. They could work on their personal relationship later; for now it was their professional relationship that demanded her undivided attention.

Payton pushed Percy Johnson's contract to the side and picked up the yellow legal pad where she kept notes for Cedric's contract negotiation. It had just occurred to her that his performance in today's game had put him close to breaking into the NFL's top twenty all-time rushing yardage. They could demand an extra bonus if Cedric passed that threshold next year.

Her BlackBerry buzzed atop her coffee table. Payton's stomach instantly tightened, as it did every time she got an email or text message these days. But the message wasn't from Cedric, just an email from the Twitter service she'd signed up for. It alerted her any time the volume of internet chatter surrounding Cedric's name on the social networking site passed a certain number.

A tiny burst of excitement fluttered in Payton's stomach as she read the tweets—the Twitter messages people were posting regarding Cedric's stellar performance in today's game. Despite the loss, Sabers fans were ready to nominate the team's running back for the NFL Hall of Fame.

As Payton came across a tweet from a columnist for one of the biggest online sports magazines, the fluttering in her stomach stopped and was replaced by a feeling of dread the size of a boulder. She scrolled through the messages the columnist had posted. He claimed the insider information came from a source deep within the Sabers organization.

*Cedric Reeves joins Hayes Entertainment Management Co.*

*M. Hayes will take C. Reeves to the next level.*

Payton blinked several times, unable to digest what she was reading. She clicked on the pages of several other sportswriters who were also reporting that Cedric had signed with mega-agent Marvin Hayes.

Cedric had fired her.

Payton shot up from the couch, grabbed her coat and headed out the door. It wasn't until she'd made it to Manhattan that it occurred to her that she should call to make sure Cedric was at his home, though he probably would not have answered the phone anyway. Chances were she would be stopped at the front desk of his building again but she'd cross that obstacle when she came to it.

By some miracle, she found an open parking space on the street. Payton parked at a meter two blocks from the building. Whether it was luck, fate or some higher power, Payton didn't know, but something was working in her favor. As she approached the entrance to the building's parking garage, the gates opened and a black Lincoln Navigator eased out. Payton stared right into Cedric's eyes through the driver's side window. The overwhelming rush of hurt that crashed through her at the sight of him was enough to bring her to her knees.

How had they ended up here?

The window lowered. He didn't say anything, just stared back at her.

"When were you going to tell me I was no longer your agent?" Payton asked.

The gate opened and another car pulled up and honked.

Cedric motioned with his head. "Get in."

Payton hesitated for a second before jogging around the car and slipping into the passenger side. The interior was nice and toasty, but the atmosphere between her and Cedric was as icy as the cold New York day.

He took a left, his hands tight on the wheel. They drove along the streets of the Upper West Side in the lighter Sunday afternoon traffic. After a solid five minutes of silence, Cedric finally spoke.

"I was on my way to your place. I didn't want to do this over the phone."

The dread that had sunk into Payton's bones multiplied, spreading throughout her entire body.

"Do what?" she asked, a heart-rending ache crushing her chest before he could even speak his next words.

"I want to exercise the exit clause in our contract."

Payton pushed back the threat of tears that clogged her throat. She would jump out of this moving vehicle before she allowed him to see her cry. Yet the urge to do so was so overwhelming, she wasn't sure her will was strong enough to stop the tears from flowing. Forget being a professional; this cut through the business persona, straight to the core of the woman who had fallen in love with him.

"I'm sorry," Cedric said. "I really am, Payton. I didn't want it to end like this, but I'm thinking about my career. Marvin Hayes is a legend. I don't care how much you prepare, you could never get me the kind of deal he'll be able to negotiate. Just his name adds another twenty-five percent to my bottom line."

"I know the kind of clout Marvin Hayes wields, Cedric." And she did. Hayes was the kind of agent others in the business aspired to be, and he rarely took on new clients. Cedric would be a fool not to sign with him. "It's not that you signed a contract with him," Payton continued. "It's that you didn't bother to tell me. After everything we've been through, you didn't even bother to *tell* me you were done with me."

"I haven't signed with him yet," he said.

"But you're going to."

A pause, then, "Yes."

Hurt wrapped around her heart like a fist, squeezing it in a vise grip. Somehow, Payton managed to pull herself together. Emotions had no place here. How could she tout her professionalism if she became this disheartened when she lost a client? It was a part of the business.

But Cedric wasn't just a client. She loved him.

And she was losing him.

"This is strictly business, Payton. I know what you're thinking, but it doesn't have anything to do with what happened between us after the bar fight incident. I know I've been a jerk since then, but I needed to clear my head and focus on the game. That's why I haven't been in touch."

"Well, it sounds as if there's no reason for you to be in touch now," she managed to say while keeping her emotions contained.

They pulled up to the traffic light a block away from

his building. In more ways than one they had come full circle, landing right back where they'd started.

Cedric stared at her. "Is that how you want it?"

No. Not at all. But what else was there to say?

With a nod, Payton said, "That's how it has to be."

# Chapter 16

"Can you hold one minute, Mr. Myers?" Payton switched the first phone to her other ear as she answered her other one. "Percy, I can't talk right now, but I promise I'll call you back in an hour." She switched back. "Yes, Mr. Myers. I apologize for that."

She'd once envied agents who needed to walk around with multiple cell phones on their hips. Who knew the juggle would be such a pain in the butt?

Payton finished up her conversation with the head of the marketing division at Pump You Up Energy Bars—the new super food that promised both energy and muscles. It was the perfect product for a hefty lineman to endorse. She would call Percy Johnson—whom she'd realized ten minutes after signing would be the kind of client who needed his hand held—and let him know the call had gone well. Later.

Right now, she had a meeting with the Sabers starting quarterback, Mark Landon, who was rethinking his plans to retire now that the Sabers season was over.

Payton entered the same Starbucks where she'd convinced Cedric to sign with Mosely Sports Management and greeted Mark with a smile. An hour later, she walked out without having signed the quarterback to her roster.

As soon as she learned of the multiple concussions the Sabers had managed to keep under wraps, Payton knew Mark Landon would never play another game of professional football. He'd called her because his current agent, a man Payton knew only by reputation, refused Mark's request to negotiate another one-year deal with the Sabers. Mark wanted a ring, but after five concussions over his eleven years in the league, the risk was just too high.

Another agent probably would have taken him on, collected a percentage of the eight-figure salary a quarterback with Mark Landon's experience would fetch and then hoped he didn't take another blow to the head. But Payton refused to be just another agent. Her clients' well-beings would always come before money.

She reached in her purse for BlackBerry number one, intending to call Percy, but the phone rang. Payton paused as she stared at the familiar name and number that lit up the screen. At first she wasn't sure she should answer it, but she tossed the thought out of her head. She was through running away.

"Hello, Cedric," she answered, walking to her car.

"Hi," he replied. "Congratulations on signing Percy Johnson and Luke Davenport," he said, referring to the kicker she'd signed last week.

"Thank you," Payton said. Not too keen on beating around the bush, she came right out and asked, "What do you want, Cedric?"

He was silent for a moment, uncertainty buzzing across the phone line.

"I want my agent to meet me at the Sabers facility tomorrow to negotiate my contract," he answered.

Payton paused with her hand on her car door.

"What does that have to do with me?"

"You're still my agent," he said. "You never signed anything dissolving our contract, did you?"

"I..." No, she hadn't. In the weeks that had passed since she'd learned of his talks with Marvin Hayes, she'd acquired three new clients and had been too busy to realize she had never received the papers from Cedric exercising the exit clause of their contract.

"You're a lawyer," he continued. "You should know that both parties have to sign the papers agreeing to end the relationship."

"Of course, I know that," Payton said. What she didn't know is why he had never sent the papers. "Cedric, what's going on here? Why isn't Hayes negotiating your contract?"

"Because he's not my agent," he answered. "I couldn't do it, Payton. You took a chance on me when no one else would."

"But you were right. I can never get you the kind of deal Marvin Hayes will. Call him back and beg him to reconsider. You would be crazy not to."

"Some things are more important than money," he answered. "Loyalty being one of them." He paused. "Love being another."

Payton slumped against the side of her car, clutching the phone to her ear as if it were a lifeline. Her heart swelled until it ached.

"I love you, too, Cedric."

"Then meet me tomorrow. Eleven a.m. at the Sabers's front offices."

"I'll be there."

Cedric turned to his brother, the smile on his face uncontainable. He bounced his phone from one hand to the other, exhilaration rushing through his veins.

"Did you…fix…what was…broken?" Derek managed to get out.

"I did," Cedric nodded. "I don't know how but I think I fixed it."

He patted his knee and motioned for Derek, who lay prone on the floor, to lift his leg. "Up here," Cedric directed. In subtle, incremental movements, he edged his brother's bent knee toward his chest, then eased it back into resting position.

"You like it here at Marshall's Place, right?" Cedric asked.

"Yes," Derek answered.

"Good, because I think you're going to be here for a while. And the best thing is I'll only be an hour away for a long time to come. Next week, I'm going to bring someone here for you to meet. You'll like her."

"Is she…your girlfriend?"

"Yeah," Cedric answered. "She is."

"I…have a…girlfriend," Derek proclaimed.

"You do?"

"Yes. I'm…gonna…gonna marry her."

"That right?" Cedric chuckled. He leaned over and

lifted his brother's other leg up. "Guess what? I'm going to marry my girlfriend, too. She just doesn't know it yet."

Cedric sat behind the wheel of his SUV, watching the winding driveway that led to the Sabers's front offices the way a hawk eyed his dinner. It was ten forty-five a.m. and Payton had yet to show. Every time his brain tried to conjure the thought that she'd stood him up, he put a stop to it. She would never do that. If there was anything he'd learned about Payton over these months, it was that she was a professional. She'd agreed to negotiate his contract. She wouldn't let him down.

Just then Cedric spotted her sedan coming down the drive at a much higher rate of speed than the posted fifteen mph speed limit. She found an open spot three slots down from where he'd parked. Cedric met her at the rear of her car.

"Sorry I'm late," she said. "Someone ran into a fire hydrant right outside of my building. Traffic was a nightmare."

"The important thing is that you made it with—" he looked at his watch "—nine minutes to spare."

"Oh, God. We need to get in there." She started walking, then stopped. Took a breath. "Okay, I need to calm down."

The transformation was stunning. With a few deep breaths, she went from harried to completely composed. The ultimate professional. Payton looked him in the eye, a small smile perched on her lips.

"Are you ready?" she asked.

"Oh, yeah, baby." Cedric rubbed his hands together. "Let's do this."

Over the past several months, Cedric had tried to

imagine how Payton would handle the forces of nature also known as Sabers upper management. It had taken less than ten minutes of negotiation to realize his worries had been unwarranted. Milton Crawford was a rain shower compared to Typhoon Payton. She didn't try the usual tactics, the strong-arming, the hostility and shouting Gus was prone to do.

Payton's method was much more effective. She'd turned the tables on Crawford and the rest of Sabers management. Instead of her trying to convince them that Cedric was good for the team, Crawford was listing all the reasons Cedric should stay with the Sabers.

She sat at the conference table with her fingers crossed, those sexy shoulders squared. She was strength and power and knowledge all wrapped up in a smoking-hot business suit that Cedric couldn't wait to peel from her body. She waited for Tom Rutledge, the team's general manager, to finish his diatribe about where the Sabers were headed as a franchise and how Cedric was an integral part of it. Then she went in for the kill.

"We all know what Cedric means to this team," she said. "We also know that after the season he just had, teams around the league have been ringing my phone night and day."

*They had?*

"However, Cedric wants to remain a Saber," she continued. "He's a part of this community and has embraced the fans just as much as they have embraced him. But he also wants to win a ring," she stated.

"We all want that," Rutledge said.

"But you've come up short for the past four years. Cedric has done his part. In fact, he went above and beyond this year. Yet, once again, the Sabers started their off-season early."

Payton lifted the teal coffee mug with the roaring Sabers logo and took a slow sip.

"So, here's what we're willing to do," she announced after a stretch of silence Cedric knew was deliberate. The woman was good at her job. "We're willing to leave some money on the table, and not ask for the seventy million we'd originally planned to demand, *if* the Sabers are willing to bring in talent to help take this team to the next level."

Cedric tried to keep the surprise from showing on his face. Where had she gotten that number? The most he'd expected was forty million, tops, for the four-year extension deal the Sabers had offered.

"Some things are more important to Cedric than money." She glanced over at him and gave him a slight nod. "Cedric wants to give these fans the championship they deserve, and if that means a smaller contract for him, so be it."

She was brilliant. Cedric had to fight the urge to jump out of his chair and wrap his arms around her.

"My client is willing to settle for fifty-two million for the next four years," Payton said. "Along with the performance incentives, of course."

Cedric sat in awe as Sabers upper management pounced on the offer. Just like that, Payton had gotten him an additional twelve million dollars and convinced two of the toughest negotiators in the National Football League that they'd somehow gotten a steal. How could he not love this woman?

The meeting ended with a round of handshakes— much better than the bloodshed Cedric had been anticipating. He held the door open for Payton and followed her out of the conference room, staring at how the fitted jacket hugged her curves. She looked just as good from the back as she did from the front.

When they exited the building's front doors, Payton grabbed hold of his hand and squeezed hard, her purposeful strides taking them to his SUV. When they arrived at the vehicle, she turned to him and let out a yelp.

"Did I really just do that?" she asked after a deep breath.

"Yes, you did. You were freaking amazing in there."

"I know," she said, her expressive eyes wide with wonder and pride. "It felt so natural. God, Cedric, it felt so *right*."

"When you're doing what you're meant to do, it usually does feel right."

She pulled him close and surrounded him with her arms, holding tight.

"Thank you," she whispered in his ear. "I never would have gotten through that without you by my side."

Cedric pulled back and stared into her eyes. "Are you kidding me? You didn't need me back there. You were in control from the minute you walked into that conference room."

"Only because you were there to encourage me. You and my dad," she said, closing her eyes tight. When she opened them they glistened with tears. "I felt him with me the entire time."

"He's going to be with you always, Payton." Cedric took her hand and dropped down to one knee. "And if you'll have me, so will I. Marry me, Payton."

Her chest expanded and the tears began to flow in earnest. She tried to speak, but being coherent apparently wasn't high on her priority list at the moment. It didn't matter. The love shining through her eyes was all the answer he needed.

But then with a teary laugh she spoke the words that changed his life forever.

"Yes, Cedric. Yes, I'll marry you."

## Chapter 17

Payton's back bowed as delicious pleasure coursed throughout her bloodstream. Cedric's strong hands slid down to grip her hips before snaking to the small of her back, then over her butt. His fingers sank into her flesh, clutching her to him, guiding the erotic rhythm of their lovemaking as he pumped harder and harder.

She came again in a rush of skin-tingling pleasure, satisfaction radiating from every fiber of her being. She collapsed atop Cedric, relishing the warmth of his sweat-slicked skin against her breasts. He rubbed his hands up and down her back, settling once again on her rear end. He held her in place, his body still hard inside of her.

Payton found the strength to open her eyes. She tilted her head to the side, and spoke into the curve of his jaw. "I can stand to do that every night for the next fifty years. How about you?"

"Fifty? You plan on tiring out on me that soon?"

Payton nipped his skin with a playful bite, then rolled off of him. She settled her back against his chest and brought his arms across her stomach. Ribbons of contentment twisted around her heart. No one should be so lucky, but somehow she was.

"I'm nervous about meeting your brother tomorrow," Payton admitted after a few minutes of comfortable silence. "What if he doesn't like me?"

"You don't have to worry about that. He likes pretty women. We are twins, after all."

"That's cause for concern right there." She laughed. "I'm not sure the world can handle more than one of you."

He chuckled and tightened his hold, running his palm up and down her arm.

"I don't want you to feel anxious. Derek is going to love you and so will the rest of my family. I can't wait to take you to Philadelphia to meet my mom. She's excited about meeting you."

"You sound so confident."

"I am. For the first time in a long time, I'm not worried about anything."

He rolled her onto her back and began to move inside her again.

Twenty minutes later, Payton lay prone on Cedric's king-size bed, fairly certain she would not be able to walk for at least a full twenty-four hours. She needed several minutes of rest before she could gather the strength to turn onto her side and prop her chin on her upturned palm.

"Who knew such a wild woman was hiding underneath those business suits?" Cedric's devilish grin made her entire body blush.

"Be honest," Payton said. "Did you think we would

end up here when you agreed to take me on as your agent?"

"Did I *think* it would happen? No. Did I *want* it to happen?" He leaned over and placed a gentle peck on the tip of her nose. "Absolutely."

"I didn't," she said. "I thought getting involved with you would be the worst thing for my career."

"But now you see that you had nothing to worry about, right?"

She nodded. "Who knew I was getting such a sweet deal when I signed you to Mosely Sports Management?"

"You may think your deal was sweet, but I got the best thing out of all of this," he said.

A single brow quirked up. "And just what is that?" Payton asked.

He melted her heart with a single word.

"You."

\* \* \* \* \*

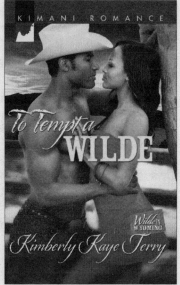

# REQUEST YOUR FREE BOOKS!

## 2 FREE NOVELS
## PLUS 2 FREE GIFTS!

KIMANI™
ROMANCE

### Love's ultimate destination!

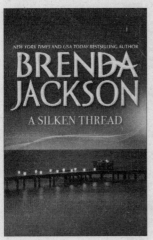